HILL COUNTRY MYSTERIES

A FRESH Brew

A Dragon Cozy Mystery

International Bestseller

Verena DeLuca

Copyright

A Fresh Brew

Published by Aconite Cafe
P.O. Box 63
Marble Falls, TX 78654

www.AconiteCafe.com

Cover by Aconite Cafe

ISBN: 9798730365643

Author's Notes

This series is one that I never knew I needed to write, it has done wonders for releasing my sass. At times it can be too much for the real world to handle, but in Aconite Cafe, no sass is too far. We've done our best to model Hailey and Azure after our own personal quirks, and from feedback of those that know us, I hope we nailed it.

Working as a team has brought us closer together. Our relationship was amazingly unique before this series venture, but now it is at a whole new level. When we are not busy homeschooling our daughter, we spend our time discussing the next mystery, or how to work inside jokes into the text. Each character in this series gets discussed in so much depth, they often feel like real people to us.

I am truly grateful to you for choosing this cozy mystery above all the others out there. If there is ever something you'd like to know about our world, please reach out! We'd be glad to work in any questions or world building into the next book!

Next on my list is A Bitter Cup, and it promises to be a fun mystery full of snark. After hearing back from readers, I have decided to double down on Azure's personality.

Marble Falls in real life, is the best small town in all of Texas. And I consider myself blessed to be able to live there with my family. We moved from Austin to downsize our lifestyle, and focus on those things that matter most, Family & Books! Our new lifestyle in a tiny house, with two cats and a massive yard to play in, means that we are never bored.

Our life is not perfect, I doubt anyone's is, but it is as close as we have ever been to perfection! Family, coffee, books, and

beautiful nature all around us, I do not know what more I could ask for.

Our next big family adventure is to move from our tiny house into a forty foot sailboat, and explore the Caribbean. If all goes well, we plan to buy a run-down boat, and rebuild it as a family. Frugality is a way of life for us. The best part is, we will be able to write while we travel.

There is nothing that will stop us from writing.

Thank you again for reading! I hope you loved the story and the characters. You can expect a book per month from us, for the foreseeable future.

To Jess,

My first reader.

Monday, February 17th

My coffee tasted bitter, and not because of the blended latte I brewed that morning. With a café at my disposal and at least two decades' worth of practice, I could not recall the last time I had a bitter cup of coffee.

I guess standing in the front row of my Great-Aunt Tona's funeral left life with a bitter aftertaste. The sun hid behind the clouds, but the humidity of the day ensured I was sweating in my black dress—a knee-length, fitted thrift-store special with a flowing sheer overlay, picked out by Tona herself.

All of my favorite outfits had been gifts from her. She had a great fashion sense and knew how to accentuate my rectangular frame. If it were left to me, I would only wear jeans with comfortable shirts.

Did she know I would wear it to her funeral when she bought it?

I pushed the sadness creeping up out of my mind and shifted Tona's beloved cat Azure to my other shoulder. His fluff butt weighed more than it appeared. The balancing act of holding a full-grown male cat and a cup of coffee made me rethink the funeral home's offer to provide folding chairs during the service.

Or maybe I should not have agreed to follow through with this particular will request?

Azure snuggled deeper into my neck, and sweat rolled down my back between my shoulder blades. He was one of the fluffiest black cats I knew of, and while his fur was soft and cozy, it was more like holding a furnace than a cat.

Might not have been the best idea to wear the floppy-brim black hat, but it sure had stopped the wandering eyes.

Why does death turn the grieving into a spectacle?

Yup, my eyes are puffy and bloodshot Laura. You can stop craning your neck to analyze my level of grief any time now.

I rolled my eyes and sighed.

If only there was a way for me to slip away unnoticed and avoid the after-funeral precession of people telling me she was in a better place. Or how I was strong and would find a new normal.

Unfortunately, I knew it would be impossible for the locals to let someone grieve in private. A bunch of soggy tea drinkers, the lot of them. Here was the better place. Tona needed to be here, with me.

I was not ready to say goodbye. We should have had forty more years, at least. But no, a clumsy accident that I bet I could have prevented had I offered to stay and help roast beans took her from me. Why had I not at least offered to stay? Like I had plans for Valentine's . . . yeah right.

As tears began to wet my cheeks for the umpteenth time that weekend, I took in a deep breath and counted to ten. I tried my

best to concentrate on Azure's purrs to steady myself. It was too hot to be letting my thoughts get me more worked up than I already was.

I guess I should be thankful I remembered to put my tangled mess of chestnut hair into a low messy bun. Living in Texas with thick shoulder-length hair was a death sentence. In college, I discovered shaving up two inches from the nape of my neck was my best defense against the constant mid-eighties to low hundreds.

". . . passing of our beloved Tona Simpson leaves many in despair . . ." the pastor droned on.

It was strange to have him lead the funeral since I was not a churchgoer myself. But if I was being honest, Tona was never big on church either, and I doubt they had spoken more than a handful of times. In a small town like Marble Falls, everyone knew everyone. To be a part of the community, one had to follow tradition.

Thankfully, Tona had her funeral planned out down to the bean. It would not have flowed as well otherwise. The thought of all the strange details in her will made me crack a smile. Leave it to her to pick the grave furthest from the entrance—always adding spice to everything she touched even after death.

The love for her was palpable. So many people gathered in the smallest of spaces at the oldest part of the cemetery.

How did she even manage this spot?

Too bad February in Central Texas meant the grass and flowers were still dormant. Tona would have loved a burial with the wildflowers in full bloom.

Across the grave, Victoria—Tona's go-to bakery owner for pastries for as long as I could remember—stood with a group of eccentric women. Aside from the bright clothes they chose to wear to a funeral, the cats circling their feet stood out like a sore thumb.

What is the deal with cats at funerals?

Tona requested Azure's presence, and given her status as a local spinster cat lady, I did not think twice about it. But I had not expected to see others bringing cats. Their constant whispering made me uneasy. Why come to a funeral just to have a conversation during the service?

I could not imagine what would bring a wide age range of women together. Unless, no, there was no way Tona was in a cat group without telling me. Right? She would have told me.

Our relationship was a mix of best friends to mother and daughter. I told her everything and had always thought she was just as open with me.

But, looking at the cats, it was the strangest thing to see so many breed variations in one spot. Had to be a reason for their presence that tied back to Tona. Maybe I could ask Victoria, but that would mean socializing, and that was for sure something I was not ready to do yet. I shuddered, realizing there was a naked cat in the bunch. They were so creepy. A few of the breeds I had only ever seen in photos.

From the way the women stood so close to one another, they had to know each other well. Not that I could recall ever seeing any of them around town. Well, one of the younger ones might have gone to high school with me, but I could not be sure from this distance.

The pastor's speech ended, and it was time for the lowering of Tona's body into the ground to meet her final resting place. Azure leaped out of my arms and darted toward the other cats as they gathered around Tona's casket, as if to mourn her passing. His black fur matched the somber air of the place.

I promised myself I would not cry. Not again. I had buried my face in my pillow all weekend, bawling my eyes out.

If not for Aubrey checking up on me, I would have starved. As a mother of two children, she knew how to cook the best casseroles. Closest I came to cooking was adding chocolate chips to premade cinnamon rolls.

"Hailey." Aubrey placed her hand upon my shoulder. "We're going now. Can you make it home okay?"

"Yeah," I said, more out of instinct than actual conviction.

"I can stay if you want. Just say the word," Aubrey said.

"No." I cleared my throat. She had done so much already. "Y'all go on, enjoy the day. It's what Tona would have wanted."

"Okay, if you're sure," Aubrey said. Her voice made it clear she was hesitant to leave me alone.

"I'm okay. I'll call you as soon as I get back to the café," I said, with as steady of a voice as I could muster.

"You better." She gave my shoulders a gentle hug. "Love you."

"Love you too. Thanks for everything. Couldn't have gotten through this weekend without you."

"Whatever, like I would leave you to starve to death. Probably would have only taken one meal with how you eat."

I took my eyes off the cats to look at her. I gave her a smirk and meant to give a sarcastic retort, but a flash of sparks from the casket area drew me back.

What the tea was that?

Each cat sat a foot apart from the next, surrounding the grave. Did they know who was in the casket? The seven of them were as still as the dead with their heads bowed as if in prayer for Tona.

Stop being crazy, Hailey. Cats are not sapient.

I forced myself to look at anything else. I could not recall if Aubrey had said something before she walked away, kids in tow. It seemed like half the town had shown up, not that my own parents bothered to make the trip. I rolled my eyes at the thought as I watched the sea of people make the hike back to the cars and bikes along the perimeter of the cemetery road.

Personally, I was not affected by their absence. Tona was my mother's aunt, but they were never close. All of my earliest childhood memories are of hanging out with Tona while my parents worked. After I completed high school, they moved to Dallas. From then on, our only communication was phone calls on holidays. Being in my early thirties, I was satisfied with the state of our relationship. Besides, Tona was all the family I had needed.

Sheriff William Brooks had come—of course—as he was Aubrey's husband. But so too did his deputy, Barry West, or as I preferred to call him, "Barry Bear." If those adorable brown bears were human, they would resemble Barry.

Today he had his wavy shoulder-length chestnut hair pulled back into a man bun, but the natural highlights still caught the sun. His golden muscular skin glistened from the humidity, putting a needed smile on my face. Police uniforms never looked so good to me. He must be on duty. I loved how defined his dimples became each time I called him by the nickname.

To my shock, Sam showed up. He and Tona had been feuding for twenty years. Tona always claimed it was over the superior caffeinated drink: tea or coffee. Coffee, obviously! But her under-the-breath comments toward him made me feel that there was a bigger dispute going on.

His grandson, Tanner, must have stayed back to operate the tea shop. It would obviously be blasphemy to miss out on a day of commerce, especially when the competition was closed to mourn the loss of the owner.

In a moment of pure awkwardness, my eyes locked with Sam's, and he quickly looked away. I rolled my eyes to resist the urge to walk over and tell him off. The nerve of that guy. Showing up here of all places.

I took another sip from my travel mug, only to find my nose tightened from the bitter taste. Might have to add sugar to the next cup. It was not as if I would stop drinking coffee. If Tona was not already dead, the idea would surely have killed her. Not to mention the shock it would put my body into.

Nope, coffee was my life, my religion, my blood. I just needed to get home.

As people passed me, they continued to touch my shoulder, offering condolences. The constant human contact made me itch. It was far past my usual comfort level. I needed them to clear out so I could have my time with Tona.

". . . brain . . . did you hear . . . fail . . ." Hearing snips of gossip as they passed drove me crazy. This town lived and breathed the gossip mill, but it was always hearsay, assumptions, and half-truths.

"I'm sorry for your loss," Brett said from behind me.

I turned around to face him. "Thank you."

In his outstretched hand, he held a business card for me to take.

"Your aunt and I were discussing the sale of the café. When you're ready, give me a call."

Sell the café? Never. I would rather die.

"When did she agree to sell?" *Like Tona would ever agree to something so ridiculous.*

"Um, well . . ." Brett stammered, as if he was not prepared for the question. "We hadn't settled on an exact date. We were still discussing the final price."

Victoria walked up behind me, and Brett looked over my shoulder. "We can discuss this later. Again, my condolences for your loss."

I could not be sure, but he seemed nervous at the idea of our conversation being overheard. He tripped over his own feet as he walked away. Not exactly impressive for a real estate agent. I bet he had clients falling over themselves to work with him.

"I'm so sorry." Victoria gave me a hug. "I can't even begin to imagine the pain you are going through. Tona was a ray of sunshine, and we will miss her dearly."

One of my biggest pet peeves was people touching me, and even though I had known her for years, Victoria and I were more acquaintances than friends.

"Thank you," I said.

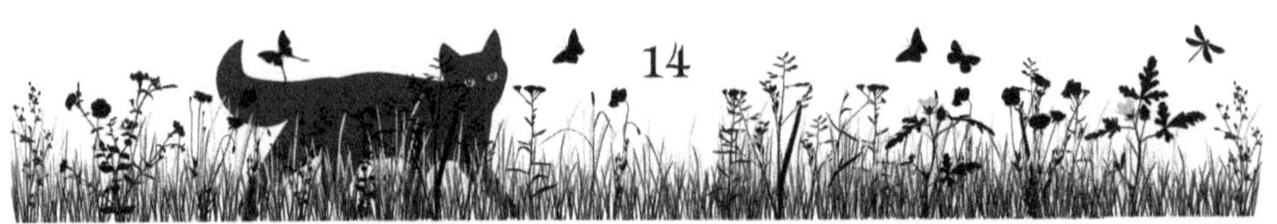

How many more times would that have to happen? Between the touching and fake sympathy, I had zero desire to attend another funeral any time soon.

"I'm sure you have enough on your mind today, so we can discuss business later," she continued. "We just wanted you to know we're here for you if you need to talk." She gestured to the crowd of cat ladies with her.

She gave me another pat on my shoulder. "If you decide to reopen the café, just give me a call, and we can go over deliveries."

I gave her a flat look—the gossip mill must be working on overdrive with all these naysayers.

The group of ladies turned to walk down the row of graves toward their parked cars, and Victoria followed.

"Oh, almost forgot," she called over her shoulder. "We'll see you Thursday, regardless."

"What? . . . Why?" I asked.

"Oh, don't worry, hon. Azure will explain." She gave me a knowing smirk and winked. "If it's too much, just let us know. Running a business can be overwhelming."

What the tea does that mean? Why does everyone think I will close the café? These crazy cat ladies were too much. Knowing Tona's quirky obsession with cats, I really was probably about to get baited into some cat cult.

I stared after the ladies, pondering over Victoria's words and the fact that there was definitely a girl I went to school with in the bunch. Cat lady groups seemed like something the elderly would be organizing. Maybe she was just driving her grandma. For the life of me, I could not recall her name. Summer or something, not that it mattered. Just another tactic to distract my mind from

Tona. Between the cats and Sam, I was a little curious to know what all Tona had been keeping to herself all these years.

If Azure thought for a second that he would continue to receive pampering like a king, he was in for a rude awakening.

As if sensing my thoughts, Azure came to my legs and began rubbing his head against me.

"Are you hungry?" I asked.

He meowed as if to say, "Yes, woman, feed me!"

"Fine, fine," I said. "Let me say goodbye to Tona, then we'll head home."

I walked up to her plot and looked down at her casket. Tona picked it out, of course, a deep blue. The longer I stared at it, the more it seemed to sparkle.

Does the paint have glitter in it? I could not recall from the viewing in the funeral home. The weekend was still a blur to me. I bowed my head and let the tears fall freely without restraint for the final time.

Tona, you were my rock. My dearest second mom. I would not be who I am today without your guidance. I hope you are watching over me because I am going to make you proud. Know that I do not believe for a second that you would want to sell the café*. Love you to the bean and back.*

Azure put his paws on my waist, kneading and stretching his back as if he wanted me to pick him up. I lifted him and cuddled my face into his warm fur as I scratched his head.

"Looks like it is just the two of us, fluffball," I said, and Azure's purrs comforted my broken heart.

I glanced back down at the casket one last time before heading to my bicycle to take Azure back to the café apartment. It put a smile on my face to see him try to curl his fat belly up in the handlebar basket.

Cats are strange.

Monday. February 17th

It was late, and I knew I needed to get to bed, but I continued to clean. When we arrived home from the funeral, Azure darted upstairs for lunch. After I fed him, he moped to the couch and had not moved since.

I figured the loss of an owner had to be just as hard on a pet, so I excused myself to the café to get it ready for tomorrow. Aunt Tona specifically stated in her will that I was to open the café right away, though I would have preferred to mope around for another few days.

Of course, she called me out before I even had the chance to mope, proving yet again that she knew me too well. At least, on the bright side, the bustle of customers would help ease my thoughts. Probably her point in writing the statement.

With it already having been closed for three days, there was a light layer of dust beginning to form. The rock-crushing factories in our area would be the death of us, no thanks to the city council.

What will they spend all that sweet tax money on when their citizens are moving out of town because of air quality?

I glanced around my home away from home.

The café was decorated in cozy browns, with a lush armchair reading area for two that greeted customers at the entrance. Then to the right, the focal point of the front windows, sat the brass bean roaster. To the average tourist, it might seem like a decorative piece, but each week Tona roasted a fresh batch of beans in it.

It was still hard to believe she did just that a few short days ago. The one thing that gave her joy would also be the thing to take her life. I had already ordered slip-proof mats for under the roaster. I could not let anyone else slip and hit their head on the rim.

Oh, tea, I would have to brush up on my roasting skills. Though, I was not sure how I was going to manage that. I doubted there were any notes around here on how to run the café without her. Tona memorized everything and never left a paper trail. I shuffled around in the drawer under the counter for a pad of paper and pen. It was time to create an operations list for the café.

I wrote *Roast a small batch to test skills* on the pad, then laid my head on the cool countertop. What else needed to be done?

To offer the most seating, Tona liked the register area in the L-shaped counter's bend, with a flap at each wall to exit the server area. I convinced her to upgrade to a tablet for orders when I came back from college. It was a hard persuasion, but she ended up loving how it opened up the counter space.

It was surreal to think it was all mine now, and it warmed my heart to know Tona trusted me enough to leave me her life's work.

I had only learned of the will days before the funeral. But Tona left me the café, which included the apartment upstairs—no more renting for me—along with everything in her bank accounts. Nearly fifty years of running the café added up to quite the estate.

Before that morning, I never gave much consideration to how much she earned. I mean, she always paid me well, and the café never went without. When I went to college, she covered everything that my scholarship did not. For my entire life, she had always given a helping hand to anyone in the community that needed it. The loss of her generosity would ripple throughout the area. I already knew it was something I was going to keep doing.

The espresso machine beside me looked brand new, though it was well over thirty years old. I must have polished the copper frame three times today. Another Tona special was the layout of the bar area.

We created drinks facing the customer to the left of the bend, giving a more friendly and inviting feel to the coffee experience. "Turning your back to a customer is unprofessional," Aunt Tona used to tell me when I was first starting out. So, the thin counter against the wall behind the bar only held decorative items and coffee-related books.

Everything was just as Tona left it, cleaned and ready for use. It was hard not to look at each piece of the café and reflect on the exact day Tona bought it or her reasons for it being where it was. This place was a living part of her.

Am I really going to be able to pick up where she left off? My heart ached just to hear her voice one last time. Why had I never recorded her saying, "Chin up, my little coffee bean; better days are brewing for you"?

As I looked down the counter, I went through the inventory in my head. The mugs sat washed and stacked, the pastry display was pristine and dust-free. *Oh tea, pastries*. I leaned my forehead onto the counter again.

How would I do this alone? I could not run the café by myself. Aunt Tona managed so many of the day-to-day affairs. I had never so much as made a supply run. She had always preferred to take care of those things, and of course, now I was circling back to the fact that she did not have a routine written anywhere that I knew of.

"The customers prefer a pretty face serving them their coffee, dear," was her go-to reason when I offered to take on more manager tasks.

I checked the minifridge under the counter and the full-size fridge in the supply room. I found just enough pastries to cover tomorrow.

I picked up the store phone—a replica antique spin dial—and flipped through the Rolodex for Victoria's bakery number. More than once, I tried to convince Aunt Tona to switch over to a computer system. She had insisted that "If it's not broke, don't fix it," and I admit, now that she was gone, there was no way I would upgrade the relic.

The answering machine picked up. "Thank you for calling The Sweet Side. We are currently closed. Please leave a detailed message, and we will call you back as soon as possible. Donut worry, we're open seven days a week from 7:00 a.m. to 1:00 p.m. Have a sugary sweet day."

"Hey Victoria, it's Hailey Morton. I know it's last minute, but if there's any way I can get a delivery tomorrow, you'd be a lifesaver. Thank you."

I hung up the phone, confident that no one would starve tomorrow. Some old men were extra grumpy before they had their cup of coffee and a freshly baked, buttery snack.

Azure meowed from upstairs, and I looked at the clock. It was already past 10:00 p.m. and no doubt past his dinnertime. It always shocked me he was not too fat to walk because Aunt Tona snuck him sweets on a daily basis. That was one thing that I was determined to change. The fluffball had to be at least twenty years old, and he could not keep up his poor diet.

I put the pad and pen back in the drawer. I guess the operations list would have to wait until tomorrow when I was not overwhelmed with customers and grief. Unless, maybe, I could call in a favor or two, find some help to at least get me through the week.

Deep down, I knew I had this. I had been preparing to take over the café my whole life. I just needed some support to get through this overly emotional state I was in. I was not too proud to ask for help when I needed it. Hopefully, Azure did not die from starvation while I begged my favorite person for reinforcements.

Aubrey and I had been best friends since kindergarten—we were Team Pink Rug. For the first day of class, my mother teased my bangs into a six-inch poof, and during recess, Tanner Wilcox followed me around, making fun of it. Until Aubrey punched him in the gut, making him cry.

We all ended up in the principal's office with our parents. My mother said Tanner did it because he liked me, but what I took away from it was Aubrey had my back. From that day forward, we were inseparable.

"Hey, how are you holding up?" Aubrey said from the other end.

"Sorry to call so late. I was finishing cleaning up the café. Just want everything to be perfect. My mind has been so scattered today. I keep circling the same thoughts without focusing on finding solutions, and now I'm rambling."

"Oh no, it's fine. It's Hailey," she said to William, most likely. "Are you okay?"

"Yeah, it's nothing serious—or emotional. It's just . . ."

I did not know how to ask.

"It's okay to ask if you need a bedtime story."

Aubrey always knew when to ease the tension.

"Real funny, Mom. Is there any way you could help me at the café tomorrow? I'm going to open in the morning, but it's always been a two-woman job, and I don't know who else to ask."

"Of course," Aubrey said. "I'll have to take the kids to school, but I can come over after that."

"You are seriously the best. I just need to get a new normal figured out. I can't thank you enough for all that you've done for me this weekend."

"Stop it. You'd do the same for me. What is family for?"

"I love you."

"Love you too," she said. "Are you sure you're fine by yourself tonight?"

"Yes, I've decided to stay here at the café, so I'll have Azure to keep me company."

"Okay, well, I'll see you tomorrow then."

"Thank you and tell William I said not to let the bedbugs bite."

She laughed. "Will do."

That took care of that fire; only ninety-nine more to go.

"MEOW!"

"All right!" I yelled. "I'll feed you. No reason to get your fur in a bunch."

I turned the single café light switch off. Double-checked that I locked the doors and climbed the stairs in the supply room to the second-floor apartment.

Azure waited impatiently at the top, looking down on me as if I was a disappointing excuse for a replacement food giver.

"I know, I know. You're a hungry fluffball." I gave him a few pats on the head while he tried to evade my touches. "You're a pretty kitty when you get feisty."

The foam on this bitter latte of a week had been realizing Aunt Tona was a hoarder. I do not mean that she liked to collect knickknacks, but that she seemed to have kept every little piece of paper from her life. Stacks and stacks of boxes filled the apartment. The bedroom was so full that I had to walk through a narrow gap to find the bed. I do not know how she slept there—the wall of boxes made me feel claustrophobic.

All weekend, apprehensive thoughts weighed on my mind at the idea of moving into Tona's space. But after going through the space, it made me realize it would need a deep clean, anyway. More time to get used to the notion of living there was a silver lining I could live with.

I opened a can of gourmet wet meat and dumped it into Azure's bowl, and he meowed as if to ask for more.

"No, sir. You don't need extra dinner."

He was lucky I found the cabinet in the kitchen dedicated to him as it is. Okay, maybe not that lucky since he was the one that put his paws on the correct door.

After a brief stare down, I made my way to my temporary sleeping area. As if my body knew it was about to get the respite it had been demanding all day, the exhaustion set in. My legs felt like they would give out underneath me at any moment.

Thankfully, the couch was clear as I had already rearranged all the boxes from the living room into a pyramid within the kitchen. It was not as if I would be using it. Coffee, I could make. Placing premade pastries in the oven at 400°F for twenty minutes, I could do. But actually *cooking* a meal? Not a chance. Best leave that to the professionals down at Ziti the Great. Italian would be perfect for lunch tomorrow.

I collapsed onto the couch, and the throw blanket that rested on the back fell upon me. In the time it took me to wiggle off my Converse, I was out.

Monday. February 17th

"What the tea, Azure!?" I screamed as I jolted awake from the shock of him jumping onto my side. My body bolted upright but instantly regretted the rush it gave my head and fell back to the couch.

After what felt like minutes, I pushed myself up against the armrest of the couch to try to clear my head. Azure's paws dug into my legs as he climbed back onto me. What time was it? Hopefully not morning already.

I drifted off before I could peek at the clock to calculate how much time I had left before my alarm would sound. I fell back into a dream only to hear a light British voice that reminded me of a college professor I once had, say, "Hailey, we must talk."

I pictured myself standing in my pajamas, fresh out of bed, in front of a class, preparing to give a presentation. But I did not have any notes and was not prepared to go. I tried to run from the room, but I was stuck, and the voice kept telling me to wake up.

Azure's toe beans pushed on my mouth, causing me to open my eyes to him standing on my face and chest. He looked down at me with the same "you are pathetic" stare as at dinner. The message was loud and clear. I was not Tona, but yet I was in his house, and he was not pleased with the turn of events. You and me both, buddy.

"We need to talk," the voice said again.

I glanced around the apartment, half-convinced I was still asleep or we were being robbed. But we were alone, so I looked back at Azure, and he backed off to sit up straight on my chest. We made eye contact, and the voice came again.

"Hailey, I have a matter that I need to bring to your attention."

Oh good, I was losing my mind. That was it. The stress and grief had broken me. The cat was speaking in my mind. Lovely. Or was I dreaming? Felt more like a dream.

I pinched my arm. Nope, not a dream. Maybe if I just left my eyes closed for a bit, the cat would go to sleep, and I could wake up like none of it happened.

"I'm no cat, Hailey," Azure transmitted.

He pawed at my cheek, only it did not feel like his adorable furred beans hitting my face.

"What the? No breakfast yet, Azure. Five more minutes."

I knew I sounded like a sleepy child, not wanting it to be a school day, but it was surely a dream, and I wanted out. I tried to concentrate on a new scene in hopes it would change me into a new dream. Relaxing by the ocean, relaxing by the ocean. The sound of waves hitting the shore and seagulls above lulled me back into what I hoped was sleep.

He butted his head against my chin. Furless and scaly. This was not happening.

I blinked, rubbed my eyes, and Azure came back into focus. Only instead of a twenty-five-pound black cat, I had a potbelly blue dragon on my chest pushing the air out of my lungs.

He jumped down onto the floor. "Apologies, but I had to get your attention."

Fantastic. He was also reading my thoughts. *TEA!*

"Look. This has been a great joke, but I'm not taking a cat-dragon-whatever seriously until I've proven that this isn't a dream."

Maybe someone spiked my coffee yesterday. It would explain why it was so bitter.

"Hailey Morton, stop being a child. This isn't a dream. I'm a dragon, you're denser than I previously observed, and we need to talk. I don't have time for your malarkey."

"Right. Okay, then answer me this. Where did you come from, and what did you do with my black fluffball?"

"Look." He shimmered into the black cat, then back to the dragon. "I. Am. Azure. I. Need. You. To. Pay. Attention."

Oh, my!

"You're a . . ." I stuttered, willing myself to wake up.

"Dragon," Azure transmitted. "That's right. You can comprehend this. Your great-aunt was my previous protector, and that honor has now passed on to you." He spoke to me as if I was slightly hard of understanding.

"But why now and what's with the sass?" Never would I have imagined the fluffers to be so snarky. "Are you sure I can't have the cat back, and we can just sleep this off?"

He eyed me with a blank stare. "It takes a few days for the bond to transfer. During which I'm the most vulnerable."

"So . . . I can't get the cat back?"

With a look that could kill, he continued, "As a dragon protector, you see my true form, along with any other dragons. For instance, Victoria and her friends from the funeral."

"You mean the crazy cat ladies?"

I looked back up at the ceiling and rolled my eyes. Nailed it. Crazy cat lady cult. *For tea's sake, Aunt Tona! You could have warned me.*

Thinking back to the funeral, I realized just how out of it I had been. I could not recall many of the people that had been in attendance, but the group of women with cats was going to be a hard image to forget. If they were a cult ...

"Tribe. It's a tribe, not a cult. Now who is being rude?" Azure interrupted my train of thought, and I rolled my eyes at him.

Whatever it was, it would explain a lot about their demeanor. It was ludicrous that I was even considering this was real life. But they were acting rather suspicious, and the cats.

"Wait, you cats were doing something at the casket! I knew it."

"Yes. We were giving Tona her last rites. The 'crazy cat ladies' are dragon protectors, and those cats are my fellow tribe mates. As such, you're now a leader of Tribe Rune, and there are rules against talking about us to even family."

I looked back down to where he sat next to the couch. Still a dragon. This was unreal. It had only been three days since I lost Tona, and already the stuff I did not know about her life could fill a library. I needed to get more sleep before I could process this.

"Right, well, I've read this book, and it never ends well, so I'm going to pass."

"Unfortunately, that is not an option. I would appreciate it if we could move out of the shock stage a bit faster than the stories you've supposedly read."

I finally forced myself to sit up. The grogginess of REM sleep interruption that filled my head cleared, turning into a low-level buzz of excitement. If this turned out to be a dream, I would be so mad. I looked at the clock by the stairs: 11:25 p.m. *Ugh.* Tomorrow would be a long day.

"All right," I said. "Let's say I believe you. This is real, you're a dragon, and I'm your protector. I have questions."

"Indubitably, but that's not the issue at hand," Azure transmitted. "We must discuss your aunt's death."

"I'm not really in the mood—"

"Not your feelings," he transmitted rather coldly. "Someone murdered your aunt."

"Well, that's . . . left field. How can you say that?"

"Your aunt wasn't clumsy. Do you really believe she hit her head on the roaster?"

"Freak accidents don't imply that the person was always clumsy. You know, kind of the reason for the freak part?"

"You know exactly what I mean. I do not need a vocabulary lesson from the likes of you."

Why would I have questioned her cause of death? Sheriff William Brooks had said it was an accident. His team investigated and found no foul play.

"These small-town cops wouldn't know a murder if it happened on their doorstep," Azure transmitted. "They're more concerned with the next football game than actual police work. Besides, when was the last murder? Ten, twenty years ago? They no doubt believed the obvious. But it was a cover-up. Someone murdered your aunt."

"I'm not saying it couldn't be true, but who would have wanted her dead? I can't think of a single enemy."

"Victoria and her used to fight all the time at the weekly tribe meetings. More than once, it forced the other protectors to separate the two of them. We should start there."

"We?"

First, he says he is a dragon, and then he starts making demands? The universe had a cruel sense of humor—handing me a dragon, and making him bossy. So funny.

Had he ever even met Victoria? That lady seemed to be a few beans short. There was no way she was out executing murder plans.

"Anyone is capable of murder with the right motivation, and with as dense as you've turned out to be, it wouldn't do to give you this mission alone."

"Rude!"

Azure stood on his hind legs and looked me square in the eyes. "You can't just scream 'rude' when you don't like what you hear. It's 'we' because Tona Simpson was the greatest protector I've ever

had. I'll not lay by and let her killer walk free while you spend the next month coming to terms with the fact that I'm a dragon."

"Fine. I'll buy this delusion for now, but I want questions answered before I decide to go along with this little wild-goose chase of yours."

"You can ask three, and this isn't a goose chase. I have evidence, and you will help me or face the consequences."

I laughed out loud. He better have evidence. Victoria, a killer, of all people. I kept laughing at his dismay. Consequences from an adorable dragon. Right, I was plum terrified of the little tike.

His plump belly stuck out between his legs as he sat waiting for my reply. If a dragon was going to be dropped in my lap, I was glad it was one of the cutest I could have ever fathomed. Though, his resting gaze gave mine a run for its money.

"As great as it is to sit here while you admire me, can we get on with it? What do you want to know?"

"Stop reading my thoughts."

"No. Hurry up. We have more important things to discuss."

"Fine. Okay, let's see. Do I get powers? Can you fly? *And*, what am I protecting you from?"

"No, yes, and death."

"Well, that was uninformative, so thanks for answering my questions," I said, looking him straight in the eyes, my level of amusement clear on my face.

He just stared at me, not a care in the world for how rude he was being. Which just annoyed me more. Who just springs "hey, I'm really a dragon" on someone and expects them to go along with it without question? Sociopaths. That's who.

A chuckle came through the connection.

"Are you finished with me? I assume at this point I need to ask permission to sleep?"

"I think Tona may have made a grave mistake," he transmitted.

"You think you're funny, but I can assure you it's just coming off as rude. I'm going back to bed."

"We need to discuss Tona's murder!" he transmitted as he sat in front of me, still as a statue.

"Look, I'll be honest. I'm not sure what I think about all of this. So since you've said your piece on the matter, I'm going back to bed." With that, I snuggled back into the couch and closed my eyes. "We can discuss this more in the morning. That is, if this all hasn't been an insane dream."

I felt him roll his eyes behind me. I had zero care left. It was time to sleep and forget about this nightmare.

My favorite person on Earth had left me, and I inherited a pretentious dragon. Awesome. What a fantastic month.

When I heard him shuffling to the bedroom, I said, "I'm hoping for the fluffball's return."

Tuesday. February 18th

"Hailey," Charlie grumbled from the bar seat, "are you going to fill this mug anytime this morning?"

It took all my self-discipline from years of barista-ing gruff old men like him to be able to reply in a pleasant tone.

"Sorry," I said as I poured into his mug from a French press I kept on the counter, full of the house blend. Drip coffee was never served at Aconite Café—another Tona rule I planned to keep.

"I know you're dealing with a loss," he said, looking as if the conversation was a bit awkward for him. "But there is no harm in taking time off."

"You know full well Tona would never allow something like her death to get in the way of serving her favorite people." I glanced around the café to ease the awkwardness. "She let me know as much in her will."

"That does not surprise me. Tona was a class act." He raised his mug in a salute to her memory.

I let the silence linger, knowing he was not looking to reminisce. Instead, he reminded me that if I was going to be open, I needed to be attentive. I had to admit, he was not wrong. My thoughts were too all over the place to stay focused.

I could only hope that none of the customers would notice the losing battle I fought all morning, attempting to not tear up at each action of running the café. Every customer that came in offered condolences, and I kept wishing I was upstairs moping instead of slinging coffee here. Between Tona and Azure, this was the last place I wanted to be, but alas, the coffee must be poured.

The bell chimed as Aubrey walked through the front door. "Hey. Sorry I'm late. The line at the school was backed up around the block today."

"Don't worry," I said. "Thanks for coming in."

Aubrey's ability to pull together a professional look with minimal effort always made me jealous. With her blonde hair—that could be washed with bar soap and turn out perfect—pulled into a high ponytail, jeans, and a caramel blouse, she looked ready to take on the café as a manager—not a barista.

I opened a counter flap parallel to the doors to let her into the serving section. Thankfully, no one was seated in the armchairs as the one closest to the counter slightly blocked the walkway. But with Tona living here and me using the back door, it was better to use the space for customers than keep it clear.

"Hope you're ready to hustle," I said, as she glanced around the café with wide eyes. "It's been crazy busy this morning."

"I mean, I thought I was, but maybe I should leave it to the professionals."

I laughed myself into a blank stare, making her smirk. Then continued in my tried-and-true deadpan voice, "I don't think I could learn necromancy fast enough to cover this rush."

"Dang it, all right. I knew I wore my tennis shoes for a reason. Let's do this."

"Sweet! Okay, the main goal of the morning rush is to get out as many mugs of coffee as possible. Only a few will want food, but that will be the easiest thing to learn today."

"Oh geez, you know I'm only an expert in drip coffee, right?"

"How dare you speak the D-word in this café?! For shame! Have the years of watching me from the counter taught you nothing?"

"Oh, great Hailey, I bow to your expertise. Please teach me the ways of coffee snobbery."

"That's more like it. You may not be up to the challenge, but we'll give you a chance, young one."

She put her hand over her heart and shook her head in an overzealous gesture of sincerity. "Thank you, thank you, gracious Bean Queen. I'll make you proud."

"You girls need to take a breath," Charlie said. "You're going to talk yourselves into oxygen deprivation."

A fresh wave of laughter came over us as I said, "Don't worry, Charlie, we've leveled up enough to handle it."

"Well, you remind me of them crazy gals on that show my daughter's obsessed with . . . fillmore . . . gilroy . . . dang it, I can't remember. Something girls. It don't matter, just sayin' all that talking's gonna get you girls lightheaded."

"Don't get me to lying. I hardly ever watch TV."

"Me neither," Aubrey said.

Charlie shook his head and went back to his newspaper.

We laughed together as we looked out over the top of the espresso machine. Nearly every table was occupied. The town had come in alongside the regulars. I hoped it was to help support me in my time of need and not to gossip.

Despite the rumors and stress of having to acclimate to being the owner, I was not worried about the fate of the café. I did not go to college just to fail at owning a well-established business.

As Aubrey took the freshly brewed French press around to fill the mugs of the counter patrons, Azure transmitted another plea for attention. "We need to go over the evidence. Ignoring me won't change the facts."

I was never going to grow accustomed to him being able to infiltrate my mind. All morning he pestered me, like a fly buzzing inside my skull. But I was still salty regarding his early morning practical joke of pretending like nothing happened the night before. He stayed in cat form all morning, not responding to me trying to talk to him but clearly looking at me like I was a loon. Then I stepped out of the shower and almost slipped on the tile at the sight of his dragon form.

But aside from that buffoonery, there were more immediate concerns. Aconite Café was not going to run itself, and Tona would rather I focus on the café. We had regulars who depended on us.

"I know exactly what Tona would want," Azure transmitted. "Us to solve her murder."

"Well, that was easy enough. So how do you brew one of these bad boys?" Aubrey asked. "And do you only brew one at a time?"

"For the most part, I do only brew one at a time to prevent lukewarm coffee." I made a disgusted face at the thought. "This is where I keep the coffee beans."

I pointed to the five-gallon bucket that was sealed with an airtight lid. It sat underneath the counter that held the large grinder.

I scooped beans onto the scale next to the grinder, 88 grams exactly.

Next, I measured out 1,350 grams of purified water.

I poured the water into our boiler and set it for 185°F before turning to Aubrey.

"It's easy enough once you get the hang of it. The main thing to learn is predicting when you'll need the next pot. I do my best to keep a pot ready at all times. But it's better to wait for a pot than have it sit around for too long."

"So, what about all the other crazy drinks?" Aubrey asked.

The water and grinder finished up, so I dumped the grounds into the French press, followed by the 185°F water. Slowly at first, to bloom the grounds and make sure no dry spots were left.

Then quickly to fill the pot to a fourth-inch from the top.

I stirred for five seconds and then lowered the press onto the grounds just enough to submerge them.

I set the timer for five minutes and let it work its magic while I verbalized the instructions to Aubrey.

"Sorry to sidetrack your question; timing is everything with a French press. All the specialty drinks are made from the espresso machine, but we'll hold off on training that."

She smiled, clearly relieved that she only had to worry about the French press. Azure tried to interrupt me again, but I blocked him. The last thing I wanted to do was think about my aunt's death, but life had a funny way of pressing the issue.

Brett swaggered his way to the counter. "It's busier than usual. Are you running a sale?"

I bet he got all the ladies, with that late forties frat boy demeanor in his step. He wore a casual grey suit and a white dress shirt, with a few too many buttons undone. The sculpted salt-and-pepper hair gave me the feeling he was really trying to hide his true age.

What a sad life.

"No," I said. "They came in for the best coffee in town. What can I get you?"

"I wanted to see if you considered my offer. It would be top dollar."

I highly doubted that, but it did not matter. I was not going to sell to him, and I was starting to think Tona had told him where he could put his offer.

"Tell him to go away," Azure transmitted.

"I'm going to," I transmitted back. "Shouldn't you be taking a nap?"

"Dragon, not cat."

"When was the last time you spoke to Tona?" I asked, curious when he made her the offer. "You said you two were finalizing the price?"

"Umm, well. That would have been Thursday, I suppose." He took a seat at the bar, and I poured him a mug of coffee. Slowly, he poured in sugar and cream.

"We were supposed to finalize over the weekend. I had a standing appointment Friday to show a ranch. Took all day. Didn't get back 'til late."

"And what price had you offered?"

"That's the thing," he said, spinning his mug. "Tona was supposed to set the price. This location is great for tourists, and with her getting on in years, she was starting to think about retiring."

Lies.

Tona would never have retired. More than once, she had joked about dying here in the café—the universe sure called her bluff on that one—serving the people she loved. Marble Falls and Aconite Café meant the world to her. There was no way she would have wanted to leave.

"Okay," I said, not wanting to call him a liar in front of all the customers who were now doing their best not to show they were listening closely. An eerie murmur settled over the packed café as we stared each other down.

"Tonight, I'll look through her paperwork and see if I can't find that offer she planned to make."

"Excellent." He drank the last of his mug and placed a five-dollar bill on the counter. "Thank you for the coffee. I look forward to hearing from you."

Brett seemed to run out of the café, almost tripping over a customer walking in. I was relieved it was another regular—the local accountant, Ben, who looked at me with raised eyebrows. I just shrugged. No doubt Brett was worried I knew there was no offer and I would call his bluff. He should have been ashamed of himself for trying to take advantage of Tona's death to buy the property, but I suppose that was to be expected from Brett Townsend, real estate agent of the year.

"He was sure in a hurry," Ben said, once he got to the counter.

"Said something about being late," I said. I made him his usual coffee to go, hoping he would not pry into the strange exit any further.

"You're going to come by this week and see me, right?"

"Yeah, yeah, I guess I need to deal with the paperwork sooner than later."

"Come on now, it won't be that bad. I'll walk you through all of it."

"Okay, but I'm holding you to that," I said with a wink as I handed him his drink.

"Let's set a date. I don't want you putting it off into next month."

"I don't know. With everything so busy here, I'll have to see when I can make time."

"Hailey Morton, I am not chopped liver, missy," Aubrey said, butting into our conversation. "She can be there whenever you need her, Ben. I've got it covered here."

"Wow! Selling out the best friend, new low." I scowled at her, but it only turned into laughter between us both.

"Friends keep us on track," Ben said, laughing at our nonsense. "I can fit you in on Friday morning. How does that sound?"

"Sounds perfect," Aubrey said, and gave my shoulders a squeeze. "No need to put off making it officially yours."

"Great, see you then. You girls have a good day now," Ben said, and took his coffee back to his office down the street.

Aubrey turned to serve another customer while I contemplated how I could get out of dealing with the paperwork of a death for another week. Couldn't I just grieve? Death sucked, and the transferring of everything from Tona to me was a paperwork nightmare that kept me up at night.

The sound of ceramic shattering broke the silence and brought me out of my contemplation. I turned around to find Aubrey sweeping up a broken mug.

"I'm so sorry. I'll pay—"

"No, you won't," I cut her off. "That first summer I started with Aunt Tona, I must have broken her entire set of mugs in the first week. You'll get the hang of it."

She smiled with relief, and I knelt to help her clean it up. "Thank you for coming in to help me."

"Of course," Aubrey said. "I'm always here for you."

"Ditto."

"What was the deal with Brett, anyway? He's such a sleaze."

"I know, right? You're not even going to believe the fact that this isn't the first time in forty-eight hours that he's brought it up."

"Shut up. There's been gossip about him and the café, but that's low."

"I'm serious. He approached me at the funeral after you left."

"Wow. Do you think Tona really wanted to sell?"

"Not a chance. I'd switch to tea if I was wrong on that."

"That'd be the day. Hopefully, he'll get the message."

"I'm starting to doubt his ability to pick up on subtle cues." I laughed.

Both times he left my presence were comical, to say the least.

"You know the crowd is probably due to the gossip chain more than anything, right?"

"I figured as much, though I'd been hoping it was to show support. What odds are they giving me?"

"Sounds like fifty to one, that you'll close up shop within the month."

"Ouch!"

"Yeah, but don't sweat it. Lexi talked to Brett last month, and he assured her that the café sale was a done deal. So she's been selling it to anyone that will listen to the idea."

"Yikes. Gotta love the small-town telephone chain."

We laughed it off together, but I still felt uneasy about others talking about my business like it was doomed.

I never had a care for small-town gossip, but Marble Falls thrived off it. An assumption could turn into fact faster than one could blink some weeks. My only connection to the drama was Aubrey. She did her best to stay out of it, but being a part of the PTA meant listening to the latest scoop each week.

"You need to show Brett he can't push you around," Azure transmitted.

"I know," I transmitted back. "I will. But this was not the time nor the place."

Tuesday, February 18th

"You'll discover a balance between a firm press and not overpacking it," I explained to Aubrey as I packed the espresso cup with the tamp. "See how the grounds are just below the line?"

"Yes." She leaned in close.

Her expression of deep concentration gave me chills. I had spent years trying to get her off drip coffee. This was going to be the moment of truth.

"This will ensure a perfect cup. Rich and smooth."

I recalled standing where Aubrey stood and Aunt Tona showing me how to make the perfect cup. The first time I had an espresso was the moment I fell in love with coffee. My father always drank Folgers drip, and I never developed a taste for it.

But after my first cup of fresh-roasted espresso, I understood the hype. The world gained more color, and I could think at double speed.

"Then what?" Aubrey asked, pulling me out of my daydream.

"Oh, right. You lock it in the machine." I demonstrated how the cup slid into the espresso machine and a quarter turn locked it in place. "Press this button for a single, and this button for a double."

I pressed the double, and we watched the machine work its magic.

"Try this," I said and handed her the cup, eager to judge her reaction.

She scrunched her nose up at the black coffee. "No sugar and milk?" And then glanced around the room and whispered, "Is this a barista prank?"

Wow, way to suck the excitement out of that moment. I deadpanned her and said, "You're such a wet tea leaf. Try it plain, just this once, then add if you still want to."

She hesitated but took a small sip of the coffee. "Oh my. It's . . ."

"Fruity?"

"Yeah. Almost like a kiwi?" She laughed at herself. "Is that silly?"

"Not at all. It's a fresh batch of Arabica from Nicaragua. They're known for the fruity notes."

She gave me a look, and I stopped myself. She knew all too well how long I could ramble on about the finer notes of coffee.

Coffee had more complexity in flavor than wines. Some of the local vintners bought their beans directly from us, and I loved to banter about whether wine or coffee had more flavor.

The bells above the front door jingled, and a new-to-me customer walked in. He was alone, in his mid-thirties, and looked lost.

Tourist.

"Do you have a tea menu?" he asked, looking at the Poison of the Week drink: Oleander Spice—cinnamon espresso, whipped cream, sugar, and freshly grated roasted hazelnut. Aunt Tona's favorite specialty coffee.

I gestured behind me to the section of the menu labeled *Tea*.

TEA

Turn around, exit café. Turn to your left and walk one block. At the intersection, turn left and walk one block. Turn left at the intersection and walk one block. Cross the intersection, and you have arrived at the tea house.

"How do you not sell tea?"

"Did you know café is French for coffee?" I said, recalling my aunt's views on his requested vile concoction. "Tea is made from a dying plant, and I'd rather experience life. So, we drink and serve coffee. No tea allowed."

Aubrey choked on her laugh and turned away, her face starting to turn red.

The man puffed up his chest and began to protest, but I pointed to the sign again and said, "I can serve you coffee, or you can go to the tea house."

"I'm going to leave you a negative review."

"Oh no, please don't. It might hurt business."

His smile let me know that my sarcastic tone had gone over his head. Tea fanatics were too much.

"Serves you right."

"Can't wait to read it. I'm already heartbroken just at the thought." I smiled and winked at him to help drive home the level of care I had for his demands.

Aunt Tona never set up a website and saw no reason to care about reviews online. As far as she was concerned, the only people looking at those were tourists, and Aconite Café was a local's establishment. We were happy to serve tourists looking for the best cup of coffee in Texas, but we were not about to become some watered-down version of ourselves to appeal to their big-city way of life.

The man shook his head the whole way out.

"Oh my gosh, Hailey," Aubrey said. "I just realized those directions won't lead him to Sereni-tea. He'll end up on the wrong side of downtown . . . in a field?"

"I know." I smiled and took a sip of espresso.

"But that's so . . . all this time, I just assumed. That's so mean."

"Sam Wilcox is a vile old man, and ew. People should thank me for helping them reconsider poor life choices!"

I forced myself to take a deep breath.

"Sorry, almost had a soapbox moment," I said. "You know all too well that Aunt Tona and Sam were enemies for as long as I can recall. There was nothing but bad blood between them, and if a little sign costs him some business, then so be it. I don't think a single person has ever come in here from their recommendation.

"Besides, didn't you hear? He'll leave a review. I'm going to print it out and frame it."

She rolled her eyes but was trying hard not to laugh.

"I'm just saying, if he feels that strongly about it, maybe he should take up a collection of charitable ducks and do tea about it."

I laughed at my own dark humor. Yet another thing I owed to my aunt. The memories of our cynical jokes brought tears to my eyes, and I was forced to duck under the counter, pretending to check on supplies, to clear them away.

"You know that makes no sense."

"Same amount of sense as walking into a coffee shop expecting tea."

"No, that's a valid point."

When I dusted myself off and stood, I saw it was after 3:00 p.m. Aubrey's children were out of school.

"You have to go," I said.

"What?" she asked, confused.

"It's already three. Your kids are probably standing outside wondering where you are."

"Oh, nonsense," she said. "We all have to line up around the block and pick up our children one by one. Worst-case scenario, I'll be the last in line."

"Don't you usually pick them up first thing?"

"Yeah. I was getting there thirty minutes before they got out and would read a book in the car. They can wait on me for a change. It won't kill them."

Her children were lucky to have such a devoted mother, and I always thought William took her for granted a little. Not that he was mean or abusive in any way, just that he left her to manage the family by herself most of the time. But I guess being a sheriff was a 24/7 job.

"So tell me the truth," Aubrey said. "How are you holding up?"

"I'm fine. Yesterday was hard. But with you here, it has really helped me not focus on everything."

"I don't want my presence to be a hindrance to your healing. No avoidance allowed, missy," Aubrey said.

"Whatever." I waved her off. "Tona's death hit me hard. I know it did. But I'm going to get through it. I mean, a part of me went with her. There is no doubt about that. But life has to go on. She taught me so much, and I'm not going to squander her memory by moping about."

"I know you will. But don't force yourself to do it alone," Aubrey said. "You've got me to fall back on."

I held my hand up in the Girl Scout salute. "I promise to not keep my emotions and healing journey to myself. You have my word."

We chuckled as Aubrey brought me in for a deep hug. There was no way I could ever repay her for the support she gave me through all of this. Now, if only I could lean on her for the dragon nonsense as well.

"Special delivery," Victoria called out as she came in.

"You're a lifesaver," I said as I walked over to drop the counter closest to the bathrooms for her.

She carried six trays stacked atop one another, with each one holding in the realm of one to two dozen depending on the treat. It was impressive to watch her maneuver it all.

Aubrey used the opening to exit the serving area and scratched Azure's head as she passed him on the armchair before leaving. *Not a cat, whatever.* It had not escaped my notice that she finished the espresso without adding anything to it. Win!

I turned to assist Tori, a plump woman in her mid-forties. She had to be a little over ten years my senior anyway, and I caught myself wondering yet again what the secret to her stamina was. She always seemed to overflow with a false air of overexcitement, and practically speed talked with a light yell for everything she said, but always managed to keep any conversation centered around her.

I always thought her appearance came off as a facade. With thick makeup lines, and hair dyed the color of a pomegranate, she was the only baker I knew that wore what I called business-club attire at all times.

I led her to the fridge and opened it so she could slide in the assorted pastries. Breakfast was going to be delicious. Fake vibe aside, she could make a mean maple pecan cinnamon roll.

"Thank you so much," I said eagerly. "They've been flying off the shelves. At least three mothers I didn't recognize came in to buy a dozen each. I think they're trying to show their support and grief at Tona's passing."

"She certainly was beloved by all," Tori said with a tone that did not match the smile plastered on her face.

Azure rubbed up against her leg. "See. I told you she didn't like Tona," he transmitted to me.

"All right, you win," I transmitted. "I'm starting to get the picture."

"Hello, Azure," Tori said in a formal tone. "How are you holding up?"

She looked around to see if the guests were watching us—they were not—and bent down to offer him a small treat from inside her pocket.

Where everyone else saw a fluffy Bombay black cat with a potbelly, we saw the truth. A small sapphire dragon. He still had a potbelly but also adorable horns, wings, and he still loved snacks.

"Butter adores these." She fed him from her palm and scratched the fluff between his cat ears.

A low purr rose from the floor as he leaned into her hand. For a dragon that insisted he was not a cat, Azure sure oversold the act.

"Well, sorry to drop and dash, but I have three more deliveries to make tonight." She grabbed a bag of beans I had prepared for her bakery's drip machine as she left the serving area.

"No worries. Thank you again."

It was a struggle not to throw her valley girl chipperness back at her.

"Of course. Anything for you, hon," she called over her shoulder. Polite, yet fake, typical Tori doublespeak. "See you Thursday."

"See you then." Her fake demeanor could totally be a mask of resentment for us. How was I just now realizing this?

I had forgotten about the meeting I was supposed to host. With all the commotion of the day, and training Aubrey, it had been pushed completely out of my mind.

"Do you believe me now?" Azure asked.

"Just because she's fake and possibly a tad resentful doesn't prove that she killed Aunt Tona, but I will admit that I'm curious."

"Good." He slinked away. "It's time for my first evening nap."

Only Azure would try to make a nap sound like some sort of royal appointment. *Not a cat? Ha! Who is he kidding?*

"Does the kitty need his beauty sleep?" I teased.

His returning transmission was less than polite.

"We are going to be working on that attitude, mister."

Tuesday, February 18th

My feet were killing me, and I had about enough of the café for one day. After Aubrey left, the entire thing became too much. I had never seen so many customers. The clock showed 5:00 p.m.—an hour before normal closing time—but I did not feel like staying open.

The front window held a simple turn sign. I flipped it over to close and walked back behind the counter. In a small town like this, the sign would be enough to let the regulars know I closed up early.

I could probably count on my hand the number of times Tona had closed early, but I pushed that out of my mind. She would understand.

Only two customers were left: Nikki, a freshman at Central Texas Community College, working on a paper; and Ty, the town flirt. The man had to be old enough to be my grandfather, but that had never stopped him from trying to butter me up.

Ty grew up in a different time and developed habits that had not aged well, but for the most part, he was harmless. It was not as if he had ever tried to grab my butt like they did in the movies. Mostly, he just invited me out to senior's night at Partners—a local honky-tonk—from time to time. I always told him I could never keep up with him. Not that it was far from the truth, as I had never danced in my life.

"Anything else?" I asked Ty as he walked to the counter.

"No, sweetie pie." He gave me his widest smile. "I'll be off. Got myself a date to keep."

"Have fun, but not too much. I don't want any late-night calls from the sheriff about bailing you out."

"Scout's honor." He held up three fingers, and the door jingled as he walked out.

It was just me and Nikki. The café was silent except for her laptop keys as she furiously typed away. I could recall the late nights spent at cafés in Austin trying to finish a paper due the next day. Though, no café in the city could replace this one.

I started my nightly cleaning, doing my best to keep the noise down, but I doubted Nikki would have noticed if I had brought out a trumpet and played.

Before I shut down the espresso machine, I poured her a to-go Americano with extra sugar. How the girl stayed so skinny, I had no idea.

But as Aunt Tona always said, "It's not our job to judge the way they take their coffee. The best we can do is offer them the finest quality of bean."

It was a quarter ’til six when Nikki packed away her laptop. I had already finished my cleaning and was reading the local magazine in an armchair.

"I'm sorry," she said. "Did I keep you late?"

"Not at all. It's not yet six. I decided to close up early and get a head start on my cleaning."

"Next time, just interrupt me."

"Nonsense. You get your paper done?"

"Was I that obvious?" Nikki asked.

"Only to someone who's done time. Some nights I still wake up in a panic thinking I have a paper due."

We laughed together.

"Thank you for letting me stay. Professor Lloyd would never forgive me if I turned it in late."

"Anytime." I held out the to-go cup. "I made you an extra coffee just in case."

She reached into her purse.

"None of that. It's on the house for closing early."

"Thank you." She took the cup from me.

"You're welcome. You pay me back by getting an A on your paper."

"I hope." She grinned nervously.

"I'm sure you'll do just fine."

I followed her to the door. "Have a good night."

"Bye."

I locked the door behind her and climbed the stairs, doing my best to ignore the burning in my feet.

All I wanted was to eat and lay down. Instead, I found Azure in the kitchen, puke all around him on the tile floor.

"What the tea?! Like I didn't do enough cleaning downstairs? I thought dragons didn't get hairballs?" I transmitted.

"We don't, you tea-tart," he transmitted back. "I've been poisoned."

"What do you mean?" I always thought cats were dramatic creatures, but they had nothing on dragons.

"Pooissonneeddd. You know, dying. I must be cursed. My last moments, and I'm doomed to spend them with an idiot."

I lightly pushed him to the side with my foot.

"That's not what I meant, and you know it!"

"Don't touch my poor stomach. Why me?" He started dry heaving again as I rolled my eyes. How did Tona live with this drama queen?

"If you were dying, you wouldn't have noticed." I crossed my arms. "Let's get you some water. I'm sure you're dehydrated."

I picked up his water bowl, rinsed it out, filled it halfway, and added in three ice cubes. When I placed it on the ground, he lapped it up in a hurry.

"Slow down," I transmitted. "If you keep that up, you'll end up making yourself sick again."

He slowed his drinking, but by the time it took me to mop the kitchen, he had finished nearly the entire bowl. Thank goodness he had the sense to keep it away from the boxes.

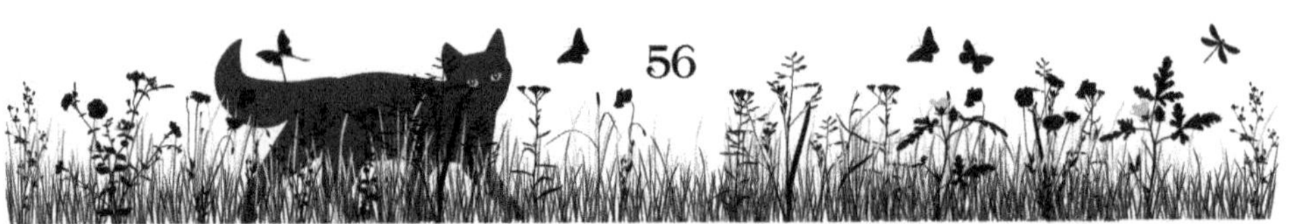

"Thank you," he transmitted and rubbed his head against my leg.

"You're welcome. Next time, why don't we try asking nicely, rather than name-calling."

He said nothing and instead walked to the couch in the living room and took up his position after shaking his wings out.

I sat next to him and scratched behind one of his horns.

"Now, instead of acting like a crazed lunatic, let's work through what you ate today. Do dragons eat out of the trash?"

"Rosemary," he transmitted, and his tone made it sound like a swear.

"Avoiding the question. Good to know. Might invest in some of those locking lids just in case. Why rosemary?"

"Is it possible for you to not be sarcastic for even one moment of your pitiful life? It's a major allergy for all dragons."

"Wow. Rude! I am being completely serious right now. Who—"

"Victoria!" he transmitted over me. "Now do you see? She resented your aunt's position, and now she's tried to kill me. If I died, you'd lose your position as the head. But she's an idiot. Her and Butter would never take my place. The dragons back home wouldn't accept them as a leader."

"That's messed up. I should get a new dragon if you die. Who made these rules?" I reached for the phone. "She is in for a rude awakening if she thinks for a seco—"

"No," Azure transmitted and nudged his head into my arm. "This is a tribal matter. We'll address it at the meeting. Besides, I have to think of the right punishment for her and Butter."

"Oh, really?"

"Welcome to leadership."

"So drama for the puking, but no drama for the culprit. Makes sense."

"Tori and Tona fought constantly," Azure transmitted while laying his head in my lap. "If it hadn't been for the tribe trade agreement, they would have never spoken to each other outside of meetings. No one will miss their passive-aggressive behavior. If I were a betting dragon, I'd point the talon at Tori.

"Given where your aunt's body was found, it would make sense they got into another argument and it turned physical. Tona was too graceful to ever trip and fall into the edge of the roaster."

I missed the cat, but even I had to admit that a dragon was not all bad. It was comforting to run my fingers over his scales.

"I get what you're saying," I transmitted, "and I agree she seems the most likely suspect, especially after intentionally poisoning you. But my gut tells me if it were an actual murder, Sam Wilcox is my bet. They hated each other for years."

"Since childhood," Azure transmitted as a slip.

"Go on?"

"No. That's your aunt's secret. It's not mine to share."

He hopped off the couch and walked toward her old room. "I've made up my mind. Go ahead and call Victoria. I know you're dying to."

"Darn straight. She needs to know. And Butter—"

"I'll deal with Butter!"

"Yes, sir!" I saluted the door.

I was not about to put myself in dragon business and end up on the wrong side of that tone. In my entire time of knowing him, I had never seen him so agitated. The fluffball I knew was lazy and uninterested. Reminded me a lot of Garfield—aside from his black fur, all I ever witnessed him do was eat and sleep. Turns out he was talking to my aunt nonstop.

I picked up the phone again, dialed Tori's personal number, and relaxed on the couch while it rang. I only thought I had left the drama in high school.

"Hello? Tori speaking."

"Tori, it's Hailey."

"Oh, don't tell me you ran out of pastries already."

"No way. I just wanted to let you know that I will not partake in the games that you and Tona were playing."

"What?"

Call me dumb, but I believed her for a second. She sounded genuinely innocent. That, or I was not ready to bring myself to believe she killed my aunt.

Tori and Tona had known each other for years. I assumed they were friends, and that was one of the key reasons I never voiced my personal distaste for Tori. It would be like Aubrey killing me.

Unthinkable.

"You poisoned Azure."

"I did not."

"Oh, okay, I must have given him a rosemary latte today. Silly me."

She stayed silent on the line, so I continued.

"Wait, I couldn't have done that—we don't keep rosemary in the café. Why would we? Coffee doesn't pair well with it."

She cleared her throat and made an uneasy laugh, but I was not about to give her a chance to deny it again.

"Help me brainstorm a minute. Who else has been in the café today and given Azure something to eat? This person would have to know that he was allergic to rosemary as it's an odd ingredient to put in treats . . . my mind is drawing a blank. Can you think of anyone?"

"Fiddlesticks," she cursed and then yelled into the distance. "Butter! That dragon will be the death of me. I am so, so, sorry, Hailey."

"I can't imagine why?" I ramped up my utter disbelief at her confession. I mean, it was dripping with sarcasm, but I doubt she noticed.

"Azure probably hasn't discussed this with you yet, but much like he will help you with roasting the beans, Butter helps me in the bakery. When I was making the batch of treats yesterday, he was passing me the ingredients. I'm such a scatterbrain, I can never remember the recipes."

"I see," I said as I heard her rustling around in what I assumed was a trash can.

"I trusted him. I mean, the treats were for him too. But since the whole batch is here in the trash . . . he and Azure have been on the outs for years. I am just beside myself that this happened."

"I might be the newest protector, but I wasn't born yesterday, Tori. You can't really expect me to believe that you had no idea?"

"Oh my," she gasped. "Azure is really laying it into Butter. Poor baby."

Dragons cannot use phones. Oh. Duh.

Of course, dragons could transmit to one another, even when they were far away. How else would they organize? I had so much left to learn about being a dragon protector.

"As I said, I will not be partaking in these childish games. Please prepare to discuss this further at the meeting," I said in my best boss voice. "Azure is formulating punishments as we speak."

I hung up the phone before she could respond. I was not sure I could maintain the act. Being a leader was never in my plans. My highest aspirations were running the café, but that should have been many years from now.

Now I find out I am bonded to a dragon who is the leader of his tribe. And somehow, that means I have become a leader of the other women?

This was not fair. Tona should have given me some level of a heads-up, right?

My eyes were hot with tears. The stress of it all was too much. Instead of swallowing them down as I had been this week, I rolled into my pillow.

How the tea was I going to do this?

Wednesday. February 19th

"I finished reading a book-drunk-worthy series last night," Aubrey said. "It's going to be one of my top reads for the year. You should give it a try. Might help you escape from reality for a bit."

Her giddy demeanor when it came to reading mimicked my own. This working together was only going to fuel our obsession.

"That's exactly what I need. I haven't read a word since Friday when I got the call," I said. Not wanting to put a damper on the mood, I followed up with a question to keep her talking. "What's it about?"

Midmorning was one of my favorite times to be at the café. Low traffic while riding the leftover high from espresso and the morning customer rush. It always made for the best time to hold conversations.

"You're going to love it! It's about a girl that loves baking and discovers she's a witch," Aubrey said, practically bouncing as she explained the plot. "The series follows her discovering her magic, baking for the royals, and solving mysteries around her newfound life. It's ten books, so that should hold you over."

"Witches, baking, and mysteries," I said. "All my favorites. Why are you spoiling me?"

"Still salty about not getting powers," I transmitted to Azure.

"I know what you're about," she said with a wink. "I brought my e-reader so we can trade while you read them."

"Good, I can use that extra salt on my lunch," Azure transmitted back.

"You are killing me with kindness." I mocked. "I'll just buy them, though. If they're as good as you say, then I want my own copies!"

"Wow. You should caveat that thought with *if* you get lunch," I transmitted.

"Fine, fine, buy them. Better for the author anyway," Aubrey said. "They are indie published."

"Like you're going to withhold food. That'll be the day," Azure transmitted.

"Perfect," I said. "I've been trying to read more indie books. I love what the internet has done for readers. More than quadrupled our reading lists."

I transmitted a maniacal laugh and smiled. I was almost succeeding at holding two conversations at once.

"No kidding, I'm going to die with a to-be-read list longer than my read list," Aubrey said.

"Same," I said, as we laughed. "As long as my to-be-read list isn't my cause of death, I'm good."

"Pretty much the main reason I don't keep physical books on my nightstand," Aubrey said.

I had to set my coffee down so I did not spill it from laughing so hard. She completed me in too many ways.

"What's the series called?" I asked.

"Duh, *Spells and Caramels* by Erin Johnson."

"Buying the whole series tonight!" I said as I wrote it on receipt paper.

Everyone needs an Aubrey. Without her, I would have spent the week a moping mess and probably would have given in to the temptation to close for a while.

The door chimed, and all I could see through the glass were flowers. Someone struggled to get the door open while balancing an elaborate bouquet of exotic blooms.

I assumed it was John or his uncle. Not that I could imagine the owner of the only floral shop in town out doing deliveries.

With only visiting Bloom a handful of times, I did not know the Greens exceptionally well. Weird how you could go to high school with someone and live in the same town with them your whole life but still not recognize them when in the grocery store.

As I pondered which Green I was going to be face-to-face with, I steadied my breath and headed around the counter to help him manage. I was in no way prepared for bereavement flowers. Hopefully, the card would not make me cry.

"Someone scheduled these for your aunt before . . ." John said once he made it into the café. "Well, we felt it best to go ahead and deliver them to you."

"Oh, my."

Here I was expecting flowers in condolence of my loss, only to be blindsided by holdovers from her life. This week was just going to continue to be shock after shock. Who would have sent Tona a bouquet? I did not know that she was dating anyone.

"Did you know about this?" I transmitted to Azure.

He refused to answer me. That little tea-tart.

"Thank you, John." I took the bouquet as his arm shook from holding them out.

"Who is it from?" Aubrey came to stand beside me.

"I don't know." I read the card, but they signed it with initials.

Tona,

Thank you for joining me at dinner last Friday. It was one of the best Valentine's I've had in a long while. A night for the record books.

I look forward to our next date.

With Love,

S.W.

"Ooh, Tona had a boyfriend!" Aubrey whispered, enthusiastically.

"Shh!" I whispered back, meeting her wide-eyed grin with one of my own. "I had no idea she was dating!"

"The things you learn about people after they pass away." She shook her head and left to refill a few mugs of coffee.

"Hey, do you think you could cover for me?" I asked once she returned and started on brewing another French press.

"Of course." Aubrey patted my shoulder. "Take as long as you need."

I was going to find a way to shower her with all the love she had been giving me. It was just too much. I was not sure I deserved such a great friend.

"You're the best."

"No, Tona was the best. No one's ever told me I was a night for the record books." She snickered through the end of her words.

"Stop it!" I said, holding back laughter as I did my best to sneak the flowers to the storeroom without drawing attention from the customers.

All the locals knew Aunt Tona—and now I—lived upstairs, but it did not make it any less awkward to walk up to the apartment in the middle of the day. At some point, I would need to deal with the apartment I had been renting, and Tona's hoard, but that was a battle for another week.

"Azure. You get your scaly butt out here," I transmitted as I stepped onto the top landing.

He slipped out from under the couch. How he fit under there with his giant belly, I would never understand.

"What do you know about this?"

"Tona wasn't just your great aunt; she also had an active social life."

"Active?" I sat the vase on the small dining table. "How active? I wasn't aware she dated. I always thought she was a homebody."

"Just because she chose not to share her evening life with you doesn't mean she didn't have one. And I would appreciate it if you left me out of it."

He stretched between steps as he walked into the kitchen to eat.

"I see your stomach is back to normal," I teased as he nibbled at the wet food in his bowl.

"I see you're as clever as a lump of wet tea."

I stuck my tongue out at him and walked to the couch.

"Could have been whoever sent this?" I said aloud, as much to myself as to Azure.

"No," he transmitted. "It was Victoria and Butter. They're a real piece of work."

"Do you have your own drama with them I should know about?" I transmitted.

"I've told you everything about Victoria."

Right, nothing more. I was not buying that at all. His focus on them in this idea of murder was too intense for there to not be more to the story.

"There have to be other suspects than just them," I said. "If not this suitor, maybe another. It could be an ex. It's always an ex."

"I'll not discuss Tona's personal life. But we shared a special bond, and if it had been some lover, I would know."

"How?"

"You'll soon discover for yourself." He strolled out of the kitchen. "As a dragon protector, we will share emotions and thoughts fluidly. For now, it's intentional, but as our bond strengthens, it will just be a part of us."

"Don't you already hear my every waking thought? How is that different?"

"Don't blame me for your inability to close your mind."

"Like I knew that was something I needed to practice," I said with a groan.

"The jury is still out on if you have the capacity to learn such a thing, but even so, you won't be able to silence everything. Especially emotionally charged moments."

"You have emotionally charged moments?"

"Don't mistake my regal nature as cold."

"Regal." I snorted.

"Even now, I still grieve the loss. If not for my obligations to the tribe, I may have chosen to follow her."

Sometimes I could really put my foot in my mouth. I picked Azure up and gave him a hug. I had been so caught up in my own loss and discovery of being a dragon protector that I had overlooked the fact that Azure just lost his closest companion.

"How long were you two bonded?" The potential murder and café craziness had been distracting me from the many questions I had about our bond.

"This year would have been fifty years. I handpicked her out of the dozen cafés this area had to offer at the time."

I could not imagine what kind of pain that would be. Would he feel the same when I passed? How would I feel if he passed?

"So Tona was the first person you'd been bonded to?"

If they were bonded for about fifty years, that would mean they met around the time Tona opened the café. The pieces were coming together on Tona's deep-seated love for coffee and running the business.

"Yes," he transmitted.

After a pause, which I thought involved sniffling, he continued. "I have wondered if that is why this loss has affected me so. But she was a remarkable person and meant a great deal to me."

"She definitely was one of a kind," I transmitted. "I can't imagine how she reacted to first discovering you."

"More professionally than you did." He cleared his throat when I huffed at the response. "But it was a business proposition, not a midnight surprise."

"Right, I can see how it would be easier to accept when one isn't woken from a dead sleep," I transmitted.

"I apologize for that. I was caught up in my thoughts. I needed to talk to you. As soon as the bond transferred enough for you to see and hear me, I couldn't wait. It is my fault for not taking a breath to realize what time it was."

"It all worked out for the best, I guess," I transmitted. "Where do you come from, anyway? No vague answers allowed."

I was hardly in the mood for another sassy retort like "my mom." At some point, he was going to have to tell me the whole story and give me the answer I sought.

"My homeland is within the cavern systems. Young dragons can study to become a tribe leader and guard one of the many cave openings around the world. Tribe Rune oversees Longhorn Caverns and a few other small openings around this area."

"What about the dragons in your tribe?"

"I handpicked each of them because of their magical talent and guard scores. Butter assured me he had changed his mind after failing his own leader training. We'd been friends since hatchlings. I trusted him to move past it. Grow into the guard role

that he excelled at. But I guess resentment often festers in those we never suspect."

"So there is more to the history between you and him?" I transmitted.

"A story for another time," he transmitted.

A deep sorrow lingered in the apartment as we sat in silence.

Dark conversations are best dealt with by a hot cup of coffee. *Tea.* I had my best friend in the universe waiting on me downstairs.

"I have to get back to the café, but I want to continue this conversation later."

"Tona would be proud of the way you've handled this week," he transmitted as he drifted off to sleep on the couch.

Did he just give me a compliment?

I stood there dumbfounded, trying to blink dust out of my eye for a moment before I headed back downstairs.

Wednesday. February 19th

"What is all of this?" I asked in desperation as I combed through the boxes left in the living room.

Maybe going through this junk after closing for the night was not the most solid idea. But with working seven days a week, there were few windows to fit it in.

"You act like Tona didn't practically raise you," Azure transmitted, clearly bored with my antics. "Why is this apartment so surprising?"

"Honestly, I can't even remember the last time I was up here," I transmitted. I opened another box to find papers and put it aside to sort later. "Had to have been before I went to college. You should know that as you never left her side as far as I can recall."

"Your whereabouts have always been the least of my concern," he transmitted. "Being a tribe leader is far too important of a job to pay attention to insignificant children."

"How the tables have turned, the unsuspecting insignificant child rose to protector of this hoard of boxes." I let out an evil cackle.

"Do you think you will have fewer belongings after a lifetime of living?" Azure transmitted.

"You do realize that for a human adult, this is not a normal amount of belongings, right?"

"Only if you realize that I have been in a mere handful of homes in the time I have lived topside—all being protectors, mind you—and this level of possessions is normal for a dragon."

How my aunt lived in a house that always looked like it was being packed up for moving was one of the many things that would forever be a mystery. I still was not fully certain what the actual apartment looked like under the boxes.

"Fine," I said out loud. His haughty tone was far past my last nerve. "As your new dragon protector, I am putting my foot down on hoarding. I will not live this way."

"Just wait," Azure transmitted.

"For what? Do you think I am so disingenuous that years from now, I will magically adapt to hoarding?"

"Dragons are hoarders. Protectors connect with us on such a deep mental level it is only natural for them to adapt to some ways of the dragon."

"I. Will. Never. Be. A. Hoarder."

"Okay, my sweet pre-roasted child, whatever helps you sleep at night."

I huffed and turned to open another box. It was pointless to continue a conversation that he was obviously all-knowing on. I

hoped he would just keep quiet but knew deep down he was only biding his time for the next moment to school me.

Secretly, I loved the debate-style conversation we were falling into. It felt great to be able to talk to someone with intelligence and then take none of my sarcasm or dry humor personally. The little tart was making losing Tona a bit more manageable. Not that I would ever let him in on that. His ego would not fit in the apartment.

"Tona was a meticulous keeper of records," Azure transmitted as he stretched out on the couch to watch me work.

"This is impossible," I transmitted. "It'll take months to go through all of these."

"Nonsense," Azure transmitted.

He hopped off the couch and brushed against me on the way to the kitchen.

"It'll take you years."

I could hear him laughing inside my mind.

The next box felt like it weighed a ton. After wrestling it to the ground, I opened it to find it full of books.

"Who stores books inside boxes?"

"Your aunt?" he transmitted in his best sarcastic tone.

"It's been so enlightening to have you here while I do this. Others should get the pleasure of having a piece of their relatives around as they clear out the belongings. Gives such great insight into the person they are now without."

"Exactly," he transmitted. "You should be thankful instead of ungrateful and rude."

"I was being sarcastic," I said aloud while shooting him a look of disdain.

A string of laughter came through the connection.

"You get way too worked up," Azure transmitted. "Take a breath. They are only boxes."

I opened the drawer of the end table that held the phone—between the couch and my aunt's chair—looking for a pen and paper to make note of the box's content. Inside was a little black book, and I recalled all the old movies we watched together. The detective always found the murderer's number inside the deceased's "little black book."

Did Aunt Tona have the killer's number? Maybe she at least had the number for the man who sent her the flowers. Who signs a love note with only their initials?

I flipped through the book, looking for anyone with the last name W and first name S. Sure enough, Samuel Wilcox. And I did not find anyone else. This was the smoking gun I had been looking for.

"It was Sam," I transmitted. "He is the only contact in Aunt Tona's little black book with the initials SW."

"That doesn't mean he killed her," Azure transmitted back. "S.W. isn't exactly rare. Sean White, Scott Whitmore . . . or they could have been having a love affair? Who knows what your aunt did with her free time?"

"No way! They hated each other. And you should know! Mr. Can't-hide-emotionally-charged-moments!"

"I never pried into her personal life," he transmitted. "We all have our secrets."

"I am still not sure that someone actually murdered her."

"I thought we were going to skip ahead to the part where you just accept that I know more than you?"

"Look," I said, crossing my arms, "obviously y'all had this great connection and all. I'm just saying I spoke to the sheriff and the coroner myself on Friday night. There was no foul play in her accident. Between their ruling and Tona being overprepared, it made it easy to get the funeral set up so quickly. If there had been even a sliver of doubt, they would have caught it. I am not saying I don't believe your fears. I just want to be sure before I go and accuse someone of murder. Does that make sense?"

"They ruled that Tona slipped and fell, hitting her head on the edge of the roaster, then the cement floor. Causing her death, right?"

"Right—"

"So please enlighten me on the evidence you would have liked them to find. What evidence is left behind when someone pushes someone, causing them to hit their head?"

"Well . . ."

"Exactly. There would be none. If it is at all possible, it would be great if you could move past the doubting me bit and just trust me. We are wasting far too much time waiting for it to dawn on you naturally."

He walked down the hall into Aunt Tona's room before I could think of a response. No doubt to take a nap on the bed. If I did not know he was a dragon, I would think he was a cat. He sure slept enough.

The box before me was full of old books, covers discolored from years of storage. The second-to-the-top book caught my eye.

It was an old yearbook from Tona's high school. Was it wrong to read it?

Regardless, I opened the front cover and flipped through the pages of black and white photos.

When I arrived at the W section, tucked between the pages was a folded sheet of paper.

To my primrose,

Your eyes are like oceans, deep and calm.

Black is your hair, like the night sky.

Fiery is our love, bright as lightning bugs.

I'll always remember of summer!

Love,

Samuel

"Ha!" I yelled out to make sure Azure heard. "I told you it's always an ex. And *ew*."

"You're such a prude," Azure transmitted back. "Now leave me be to sleep in peace."

If he kept that attitude and tone with me, I would have one homeless dragon out of my hair.

"You could help, you know," I transmitted.

"If you wish to defile the belongings of the deceased, you can do it yourself."

"It's not as if we're robbing a grave," I transmitted. "Besides, Aunt Tona left everything to me. So, I'm actually defiling my own belongings. Thank you very much!"

Great retort, Hailey.

"My sentiments exactly."

"Your mouth is on thin ice, mister!"

My evening dragged on in much the same manner. I shifted boxes around and made piles of book boxes to donate. The yearbooks I would hold on to, especially the one with Sam's letter.

After an hour's nap, Azure graced me with his presence again, requesting dinner. It was good timing because I had not realized how late it was and was starving.

I served him liver—or as my mom liked to call it, boot steak—and ordered a pizza for myself. It would feed me for the night and make the perfect breakfast in the morning.

Once we finished eating, I dove back into sorting through the boxes. Most of them were full of paperwork. Tona saved everything. Receipts, bills, flyers—it did not make a difference. Anything that came into her life went into a box. I was not sure of the best way to handle paperwork, so I made a note on my list to ask Aubrey what she thought about it tomorrow.

"Do you not keep anything? The more you complain about the stuff in here, the more curious I am about your apartment."

"We can go there if you'd like. It is nothing like this. Clean, open, calming. How a living space should be."

"Sounds horrible."

I laughed. What would he know about creating a calm environment, anyway? Stuff equals stress, more stuff, more stress. If dragons were hoarders, it would not be surprising to discover their stress levels to be high.

"You know very little about a dragon's mental capacity," Azure transmitted, interrupting my thoughts.

"Maybe you should enlighten me instead of sass me."

"A dragon's stress comes from being bonded to a protector that constantly needs to be enlightened."

"You are so pretentious. Where exactly do you think I am supposed to learn about dragons at? Is there a school I don't know about?"

"Point taken," he transmitted.

I shuffled around a few more boxes. He did have his own point. They were just boxes, and for the most part, it seemed that we could get rid of them with little fuss to the contents. I was not sure what exactly I was looking for as I went through each one, but I hoped anything important or keepsake-worthy would jump out at me.

"Are you planning to erase Tona from this building?" Azure transmitted, catching me completely off guard. His tone was genuinely interested, as opposed to the usual sass I was getting used to.

"Definitely not. Tona will always be a huge part of who I am," I transmitted.

I got up from the floor and joined him on the couch.

"If there are items that you want me to keep in the apartment or café, you just have to tell me."

"All of it."

"Not funny," I transmitted.

"It was a little funny."

We sat in silence as I ran my fingers over his scales. I took in the living room that was visible. The furniture would be staying. I had zero desire to go shopping or have any unique-to-me pieces. So, everything she had here would work fine for me.

"That will do, and maybe some of her blankets," he transmitted. "I just want to be able to connect with her for a while longer. I know her scent won't stay forever. But . . ."

When he trailed off, I spoke up, "I'm not ready to let her go either. I'm okay with this being a slow process. We can work through it together. No one knew Tona better than us. The apartment doesn't just have to be my space. It can be ours."

"Thank you," he transmitted, and promptly dozed off.

I took his sleeping as a cue for me to finish up for the night and got back to work.

By the time I shut the lights off for bed, I was proud of the dent I put into the hoard. I just had to figure out how to get the donate pile to the Library Thrift Store down the street so I would have space to go through more.

A thousand trips on my bicycle did not sound like a well-spent day. Oh well, a problem for future me.

Thursday, February 20th

The café was empty aside from Azure and I, just the way I liked it. Could do without it being near dawn, but that was a lost cause. There was always something magical about the café without customers, almost as if the coffee waited just for me.

It did not hurt that being alone also meant turning the sound system to music I could wake up to instead of the elevator specials that usually played during operating hours.

"Has anyone told you that you have a horrible taste in music?" Azure transmitted.

"There is nothing wrong with classic rock," I transmitted back, trying to push visions of AC/DC in concert. "When are you going to tell me how to block you out of my mind?"

"It's easy. Even a baby could do it. Watch me."

"You're not doing anything."

I stretched and let out a yawn as I got the espresso machine prepared and preheated.

"Azure . . ." I transmitted.

I needed to prepare for the dreaded meeting later, but first, another busy day was ahead of me. I made myself an Aconite Affogato—freshly brewed espresso poured over two scoops of vanilla bean ice cream and topped with a dash of chai spice.

I must have tried close to a thousand different coffee drinks growing up with Aunt Tona owning Aconite Café, but an Aconite Affogato—also one of the first drinks I named—had always remained my favorite. Ice cream for breakfast was the best way to start any hectic day.

"Are you ignoring me?!" I said aloud, almost in a yell.

"What? You asked me to show you how to block, didn't you?" Azure transmitted, sounding sleepy and uninterested.

"It is way too early for this level of humor."

"Which makes it the perfect time to mess with you." He sent laughter through the link.

I fought the temptation to reply. There was no response that would not lead him to continuing his antics. It was better to eat my coffee in peace.

After I was moderately caffeinated and the sugar was buzzing in my bones, I started in on opening duties by wiping the counter and tables as I pulled down the chairs for the first customers—usually older men who had long ago hung up their hats but never quite shook off their routines of morning coffee.

"One of these days, I'm going to train you to do some of this," I transmitted to Azure while I laid out the clean mugs and saucers.

Envisioning his dragon form walking around on his hind legs cleaning the café made me laugh, then the thought morphed into him as a cat being seen from the windows by a pedestrian. I about dropped the mugs I was holding as the image threatened to get the best of me. While it would be unexplainable, the situation itself would be hilarious.

"I would never act so undignified," Azure transmitted.

"Now who needs to lighten up?" I transmitted, looking over at him. I was completely jealous of his ability to maintain peak coze no matter where he lay.

Azure laid curled up in the storeroom at the foot of the oven as it baked the morning croissants. His adorable tail lightly bounced, and while I could not be one hundred percent sure, I thought he was purring to himself.

"You're not getting a croissant," I transmitted. "You might as well head back upstairs if that's all you're waiting on."

I checked the three-gallon bean container. Tonight or tomorrow, I would have to make a fresh batch. Yet another task Aunt Tona always took care of. But it could not be that hard, right? I batted away the sadness that crept in and moved on to another task.

"I'll have you know that Tona served me a pastry every morning. Besides, it's my magic that keeps this place thriving. It would behoove you to continue the tradition."

"Oh yeah?" I transmitted.

And I worried about inflating his ego. It was already too big for the café. *Ugh!*

"I'm only saying, the best coffee in Texas will not roast itself into perfection."

"And you're responsible for that?"

"Me alone," he transmitted.

"Well, then."

The oven chimed, and I rushed over to pull out the sheets of pastries.

"Grace me with a croissant, and I'll explain."

"Oh, geez . . . fine, let's hear it." I let a corner croissant fall to the ground.

By the time I had them carefully set inside the pastries display, Azure had already devoured his own. The buttery pastry left a residue behind on the scales around his mouth. It looked as if he was wearing lip gloss.

"How about—"

"No, sir," I cut him off. "You can't have another one. You gave your word, mister."

"I'm a dragon. My word is golden." He let out a small burp and curled back up in front of the oven to absorb the residual heat. "The roaster is mostly for show . . ."

"Okay?"

"Not too bright, are you? I thought that would be enough."

"Azure!"

"Oh, all right." He yawned. "I use my magical fire to roast the beans. Comes out perfect every time and infuses them with a little something extra. It's why people all across the state will drive back to get another cup. It's truly the best coffee in Texas. Maybe the US."

The sound of a trash can falling in the alley caused him to jump into a fighting stance. I ran to the back door and cracked it open to peer outside. I could not see anyone, but something had knocked our trash over. No doubt a loose herd of deer scared off by the street traffic.

William was working with the city council to do something about the overpopulation of deer. Marble Falls was a retirement-tourist community, and they spent their leisure time planting favorites for the deer. It had led to more deer than humans roaming the town.

Hunters wanted to develop an inter-town bow season—which had shown effectiveness in thinning the herds in neighboring towns—but William shut that idea down quickly. I could only imagine someone like Tanner running around the town with a bow.

"We need to discuss the murder before the meeting tonight," Azure transmitted, to put an end to my thought tangent.

"You really know how to kill a vibe," I transmitted.

"Classy."

"Too soon?"

Azure shook himself out in response and walked to the front windows to soak up the morning sun.

"As I was saying, you will have to confront Tori at tonight's meeting regarding the murder. If she did it, we will handle it as a tribe and then report it to the police."

"I'm just not convinced that Tori did it. Not to say she doesn't have the motive; it just doesn't feel right."

"We can't wait for you to have a feeling; it might be years before you come to terms with what happened."

I tried my best to transmit a blank stare.

"At some point, you have to face the fact that dragons are superior to humans."

"Fat chance of that happening."

A silence lingered between us. I just did not get why he was so dead set on Tori. All that I knew of her did not equate to killer or leader material.

"Tell me exactly why you are so sure it's Tori," I transmitted. "Where were you that night, anyway? Shouldn't you have been here with Tona?"

"For five decades, Tona and I were bonded, we had a routine, and it included radio silence unless we needed to speak with each other."

"So, you weren't at the café?"

"I will probably regret that for the rest of my life. If only I would have been here, maybe, just maybe . . ."

He went silent, and I heard sniffles from the windows. An overwhelming feeling of loss and heartbreak took over my emotions. His genuine sadness at the loss of Tona differed vastly from the front he had been putting on.

I took a seat in an armchair. "Come sit with me. You don't have to face this memory alone, you know."

"Could have fooled me," he transmitted as he hopped down from the windowsill and crawled into my lap.

"You're just as hostile."

"A quick wit does not equal hostility."

"Fine, valid point," I transmitted. "We will have to agree to take each other with an understanding that snark is who we are. Can't be too much of a difference from Tona. I did learn from the best."

"She was the best."

"In more ways than one," I transmitted.

"Her personal life is off the table."

"Don't be a wet tea leaf. Just tell me what happened that night."

"After she closed up the café, I went out for my evening prowl while she cleaned."

"You leave the café alone? What in the world for?"

"I have tribe duties to attend to, and for small prey," he transmitted and repositioned himself in my lap.

"Ew. Don't bring those back."

"I will have you know, I eat my prey whole. There is nothing to bring back."

"Gross."

"Take a look at your own food before judging another."

"Touché. So normal night outing. Then what?"

"I was across town checking on the wards surrounding the old limestone mines when I felt a jolt of emotion—"

"Wards?" He met my interruption with an intense stare.

"Continue." I gestured, zipping my lips up.

"Like I was saying," Azure continued, "the emotions hit me with such intensity that I stumbled forward. I tried to transmit to her but only received silence. I knew I was feeling a heated argument and tried to get back to the café, but my wings could only go so fast."

I raised my hand, and without transmitting my question, he answered it.

"We can glamour ourselves into cats or bats, depending on the need. So, when we go out at night to stretch our wings, people looking up would just see bats. Each tribe learns glamours native to the habitat they are living in."

I smiled at the thought of Azure looking like an adorable Mexican free-tailed bat.

"*Anyway*. Once I arrived back at the café, our connection had gone cold, and I knew what had happened. I entered the café through the cat door and saw that Tori had picked up the beans we'd bagged for her before I left.

"I was out for an hour at most. Tori had been in the café while I was out, and there isn't anyone else that made Tona's emotions run that heated. So, it has to be Tori."

The comfortable silence of thinking lingered between us. Could Tori really do it? What if it was an accident? Is it possible that a heated argument led to a physical altercation? Or could she have killed out of cold blood? There were too many possibilities.

"That is why you have to confront her," Azure continued. "You don't need to accuse her like with the poisoning. Just let her know that you know she was in the café that night. Ask her if she saw anything suspicious. We can't let Tona's killer walk free."

That was a good point. I did not need to accuse her. Just having a conversation with her about that day could not hurt anything.

"You're right," I transmitted. "If there really was a murder here, I want to know the truth. I'll do it."

"In the future, can we skip the convincing and go right to the doing?"

"Eh," I said, and then transmitted, "We'll see how this pans out."

"You're not funny."

Maybe having my own little companion could be fun. I smiled to myself for the first time that week. With a plan in sight, I was already feeling less stress.

"And to think," Azure transmitted as he snuggled deeper into my lap. "You could have been feeling this good days ago."

"You're not going to let this go, are you?"

"We'll see how this pans out." He kneaded my leg.

"You're impossible."

"If you mean impossibly brilliant," he transmitted, flashing me his brilliant sapphire eyes, "then yes."

I rolled my eyes and stood up, causing him to have to scamper off my lap with caution so he did not tumble to the floor. I did not have time to sit there and go back and forth with him.

Plenty around the café still needed my attention. Those espressos would not drink themselves.

Thursday, February 20th

"Do you want me to help open?" Aubrey asked as I opened the front door for her to come in.

"That would be great," I said, leading her back to the counter. "But you didn't have to come in early."

"Nonsense. I enjoy working here. It's been fun."

"Fun? Good to see I've lulled you into a comfortable lie." I gave her a light smile as I went to grab the last batch of pastries out of the oven—cinnamon rolls.

"Well, that's terrifying," Aubrey said. "Thirty-something years of friendship, and I'm still not always sure when you're being serious."

"Probably for the best," I said and gave her a devious smile.

"You think you're such a comedian."

"Funniest person you know."

"Okay, probably true."

Working with her would be perfection. We had less than ten minutes before the first regulars would start to show up. Not enough time to sit and enjoy one roll, but maybe enough time to use her as a sounding board for the hoard.

"If you want, start with a French press," I said as I finished the presentation of pastries. "Jeremiah only drinks black coffee. Aunt Tona spent years convincing him to switch from drip. I haven't had the patience to try pushing an espresso on him."

Aubrey chortled as she scooped the fresh beans into the grinder. "Looks like we're getting low."

"Yeah, I'll have to roast a fresh batch soon."

"You mean I'll have to roast a fresh batch," Azure transmitted.

"You nervous about it?" Aubrey asked.

"Nah, Tona was an excellent teacher," I said as Azure transmitted full belly laughter. My mental image of him going a morning without a pastry shut him up.

"Hey, help me brainstorm something?" I asked as I washed the front windows.

"Sure, as long as it's a pre-coffee topic." She laughed at her own joke.

"Oh right, my bad. Tona has a ton of paperwork upstairs. None of it looks to be café-related or important to me. Not sure what to do with it, although it's too much to just throw in the trash. But then I worry that it might end up having important numbers on it, so maybe I should find a way to shred it? What do you think?"

"Why don't you ask Ben when you see him tomorrow? I bet he knows when the town's next shred day is."

"Oh, tea! I forgot I was going to see him." I hung my head in shame as I walked back around the bar.

"Figured so. You just better get comfortable with the idea that you are going to handle all of that tomorrow because you aren't missing that appointment!"

"Yes, Mom," I said, in a sad mope of a tone.

She didn't buy it for a second, though, and shook her head. "Someone has to keep you in line."

We laughed.

I relaxed against the bar as the front door chimed. Sure enough, at eight o'clock sharp, Jeremiah opened the front door. I left the door unlocked when Aubrey came in, knowing that in all the years Jeremiah had been coming, not once had he opened the door before the designated time.

He owned the Sunrise Market—the only grocery store in town—and understood the finer details of customer hours. The market opened at 7:00 a.m., but his son and a few other employees handled the customers. I could not remember the last morning he had missed being here at the café.

I was around the counter bringing him a fresh mug before he got comfortable at his usual table.

"Good morning," I said as I placed the saucer and mug in front of him. We served French press in sixteen-ounce wide brim mugs—smaller mugs were worth tea for all I cared. There was not a mug smaller than sixteen ounces in all the building.

"Morning, Hailey. How's the new trainee working out?"

"Oh, Aubrey?" I looked back at where she was buffing clean, fresh mugs. "She's amazing. You know we've been best friends since kindergarten. Don't play."

"Well . . ." He dragged out the word. "You know what they say about mixing business and friendship."

He took a sip of coffee and sighed with enjoyment.

"It makes for the best work environment imaginable?" I said, trying my best to stay serious.

Jeremiah laughed so hard his coffee trembled in his hand. I pulled out the rag I kept tucked in my back pocket and cleaned his table before offering it for his own use. He turned it down and laughed again at himself.

"Looks like I'm not fully awake."

"Mum's the word."

I left him to drink his coffee in peace. Behind the counter, I dropped the used rag into the designated bucket and tucked in a clean one.

I looked up at Aubrey, and her face made it clear she was curious about what was so funny.

"Jeremiah thinks mixing business and friendship might be a terrible idea," I told Aubrey with a skeptical look on my face. "Might have to fire you sooner than anticipated."

"Oh whatever," she said, laughing at the idea. "I hope you told him that nothing could affect our friendship."

"Of course." I gave her a quick hug.

The doorbells jingled, and I turned around to find Brett walking in. I looked back at Aubrey with a blank stare as I walked back to the register.

"Morning Hailey, Aubrey." He walked up to the counter. "What's good today?"

"The special is Oleander Spice, Tona's favorite drink," I said. "I never make a drink a special unless I believe in it."

"Very well," Brett said. "One special, in honor of Tona."

He handed me his credit card, and his cufflinks caught my eye. The last time he was in, he seemed to be going for the unbuttoned sleeves, jock-in-a-cologne-ad vibe. He either had a client to meet today or realized I would not be swayed by swagger. I returned it while Aubrey made the drink.

"Any plans for the weekend?" I asked.

"Oh, you know," he said. "Working. As usual."

"Is that what you were doing last weekend too?"

He gave me an inquisitive look. Clearly, my best Holmes left much to be desired. But he answered all the same.

"Out at the Bucks Ranch. They're looking to sell and retire."

Aubrey handed him his drink.

"Thank you." He smiled with what I am sure he thought was his best charming smile but always seemed sleazy to me. "They're looking to sell, and I was showing it to a motivated couple from Austin. They want to get away from the bustle of the city and thought a ranch would be a fun challenge. Fell in love with the view instantly."

"So, it was a quick sell?"

"Well, no." He looked into his mug. "They haven't bought yet. It's a large purchase. But we did spend all day riding around the property on four-wheelers. Nearly ruined a pair of shoes."

"I'm sorry to hear that," I lied.

"Yeah, it's a real shame, but I'm sure they'll come around. If not, I'll find another couple eager to leave the city. Why anyone would want to live in Austin, I'll never know."

"Amen to that," Jeremiah added in.

Everyone knew that Jeremiah did not care for the town's tourists one bit, and as far as he was concerned, anyone from a city was shifty. And that was putting it delicately.

"Now, now, Jeremiah," Brett said. "We have to be welcoming. Tourism is vital to our town."

"Let them stay in their dirty city and leave us to our nature."

"So, what time did you get back?" I asked, wanting to get the conversation back on track but also not wanting to hear another one of Jeremiah's tirades.

"I spent the night," he said. "It was late, and the Bucks were accommodating."

"Dang, did you have to miss church on Sunday?"

"Oh no," he said. "That happened Friday night."

Tea leaves. That means he could not have been here that night. Azure was right.

"Think that a few more times, just until it sinks in," Azure transmitted.

"Don't be a tea-tart," I transmitted.

"If it's okay, I'll take this to go?"

"Of course," I said with a smile.

Aubrey was standing beside me with a to-go cup before I could turn around.

"Thank you," I told her as I made the transfer.

"You two take care," he said as a way of goodbye.

As soon as he was out the door, Aubrey rounded on me with wide eyes. "Since you have the grill hot, can you throw on a hamburger for me?"

"One hamburger coming right up," I said without missing a beat. "Maybe he'll think twice about firing up his own grill next time he's in the café."

"At least he didn't bring up selling again."

"I did look for anything that would correlate to Tona wanting to sell last night," I said. "It shocked me to discover that there wasn't a lick of proof to his advances."

"That is just baffling. Why on earth would Brett lie?"

We laughed together. That guy was a true piece of work.

"I can only hope this visit was a sign that he is going to put it behind him."

"You girls," Jeremiah said, "Brett ain't that bad. Can't imagine too many people are looking to sell around here. He is just doing his job."

"I guess that is true," I said. "I don't mean him any harm, just rubbed me the wrong way."

"Yeah, nothing against him and all," Aubrey said. "There was a more professional way to go about what he was after."

"Maybe so," Jeremiah said, "but if you look at it from his perspective, he probably approaches anyone that is having a business transferring hands. Can't blame the guy for working."

"You always see the best in everyone," I said, smiling at Jeremiah.

"Except out-of-towners," Aubrey laughed.

"I ain't got nothing against no one," Jeremiah said. "If they work, keep their nose clean, and respect the town, they're fine by me."

"Can't argue with that," I said.

I could not imagine life without the café or the regulars that frequented it. Half the town might bet on me closing, but there was just no way. Where else would I be if not here, having these random morning conversations? A manager at some job I hated? No thanks. Tona had the right idea. Get back into the swing of things, and let the town heal my broken heart. Everything was going to be just fine.

Aubrey handed me a fresh espresso.

"Thank you, just what I needed," I said, smiling.

"You okay?" she asked, as she leaned against the back counter beside me, espresso in hand.

"Oh yeah, just thinking about how Tona was right when she said in her will to open up the day after her funeral."

"How so?"

"I mean, if it were up to me, I'd still be laying in bed moping while eating coffee ice cream. But being here, with you and the regulars. Life couldn't get better, aside from her still being alive. She knew I was going to need the support of the town to heal from her death."

"Every day, we learn about one more thing she was the best at," Aubrey said, amused.

"If only she was here, she'd be so red at us teasing her about that card," I said.

"Like she would have even let you read it," Azure and Aubrey said in unison.

I toppled over in laughter, causing Jeremiah to look over from his paper.

How many times will I have to look forward to the two of them jinxing?

"Whating?" Azure transmitted.

"You mean to tell me the almighty Azure doesn't know what a jinx is?"

Silence.

"Well, since you asked—"

"I didn't."

"A jinx is when two people say something at the same time. Whoever says jinx first gets a Coke from the other person."

"A Coke? Why? That makes zero sense. Stop bothering me with your nonsensical malarkey."

"You say 'jinx, you owe me a Coke' I don't make the rules. I just live by them."

"Find new rules," Azure transmitted.

"Never!"

"I'm going to sleep. I can no longer subject my brain cells to this," Azure transmitted.

I mentally stuck my tongue out at him.

As the café filled up and Aubrey worked the bar, I could not help but allow myself to bask in the moment. I was going to be okay.

"And it was the last time in her life she was optimistic," Azure transmitted.

Thursday, February 20th

Shopping List

3 gal Half & Half

2 gal Whole Milk

3 gal 2% Milk

2 gal Almond Milk

Trash Bags

Compare Sweeteners to photos from café

2 gal Vanilla Bean Ice Cream

"I don't think I forgot anything," I said to Aubrey as I read through the list. "I need to make a full inventory. Tona memorized way more than I want to."

"Ooh, that sounds like a spreadsheet."

I felt her excitement in my core. Organization was our happy place.

"We're such a bunch of nerds," I said. "I'm way too giddy about organizing this place."

"I love how you can say giddy while having a deadpan tone."

"It's my most endearing quality."

"Sure it is," she said, holding back a laugh. "But seriously. Can I start on the spreadsheet while you're out?"

"It is! Ask anyone!" I gestured to the café at large. "You can use the tablet to create it or find an app. Tona literally only used it to take payments. But we can do so much more with it."

"She was the perfect mix of vintage and new age."

"Yeah, she was," I said, looking down at the tablet. "If only she had written something down every once in a while."

The warmth of Tona's memory filled me with pure happiness instead of sadness for once. It must have been due to reminiscing at work with the only person who could put a smile on my face in an instant. I was so lucky and so very thankful.

I went to the storeroom and grabbed my purse, and did one last once-over to make sure I would not forget anything. After I was certain, I popped back into the café.

"You can also start on an operation manual if you want," I said, remembering the big dreams I had before discovering the fiery truth about Tona's past.

"Oh, yes. I can create one of those. It should be easier since I am actually learning everything, opposed to you trying to make sure you write down stuff you do without thinking."

"My thoughts exactly, almost like you can read my mind," I said and shot her a side-eye glance with a smirk.

She waved me off. "No thank you. I don't have the guts to venture in there."

"That is no lie," Azure transmitted.

"Rude," I said to the both of them. I turned to walk to the back, but Azure twisted himself in my legs.

"Take me with," Azure transmitted as he rubbed up against me and meowed. "Tona took me."

"No, no, fluffball." I kneeled to pet behind his ears. "You have to stay here."

"I'll watch him." Aubrey knelt beside us and rubbed his back. "Cutest kitty in the world, aren't you, Azure?"

"I won't forget this," Azure transmitted, and meowed again. Aubrey picked him up and snuggled him close to her chest while scratching his head.

"Thank you," I said to Aubrey. "Tona's passing has really put him into a depression. Hasn't wanted to be alone."

"Aww, poor baby, I'll make sure he gets plenty of love."

She snuggled him close to her face while scratching his ears. The sight was almost too comical for me to handle. But I kept a straight face. Best to not need to explain why her snuggling a cat was hilarious.

Azure meowed his displeasure again. Like I would really bring a cat grocery shopping with me. Gross.

"As an expert in being gross, you should know I am far from gross," Azure transmitted.

"Keep it up," I transmitted to Azure. "I'll let her take you home for a play date with her kids."

"Meow," Azure purred, and snuggled into Aubrey's chest.

Good, at least the threat was enough to make him behave.

Sunrise Market was mostly empty, not that I would expect the entire town to be there at two in the afternoon on a workday.

The market differed vastly from the stores I had to battle while I was in college. My days at the University of Texas in Austin were filled with an abundance of choices and way too peopley. If there was one thing I loved most about our local market, it was the cozy feeling of the smaller store. I could walk through the entire thing and check out in fifteen minutes.

Jeremiah Johnson had owned the store for years, and he took great pride in having exactly what the town wanted and nothing more. This resulted in our chip aisle having six options and only two brands, but I could not recall anyone upset over it. They were the flavors I loved and left far more shelf room for a variety of snack options.

Aunt Tona enjoyed getting out of the café and chatting with the people she ran into at the store. Compared to me, she was a social butterfly. I had my close circle, but outside of that, I kept to myself and well out of drama's way.

Not Aunt Tona.

She always came back with the right amount to last a week and at least one interesting new fact about the people in town. Often, she would learn about a wedding or divorce, a business going under, or opening. She always knew the latest events coming to town a few months in advance so we could plan how to capitalize on them.

Over the years, we developed a statewide reputation, and we had many customers come yearly just for the coffee. Each time they remarked on how they could not find coffee as good back in their cities. We always ended up roasting more during peak tourist seasons as they would stock up to fill their pantries.

How was I going to fill her shoes? There was no way I would be able to socialize the way she did. Tourism counted for a sizeable chunk of our business, so I would have to add that to my growing list of items to evaluate when I got home.

Lost in my own worries, I turned the corner and ran my shopping cart into Sam. Had I been paying attention, I might have purposely kept walking to push him out of my way.

"Get your head out of the clouds, Hailey. This is a grocery store, not a park. Just like your great-aunt, never paying attention to anyone but yourself."

He looked ragged, as if run through the mill once or twice without my cart adding to it. Normally, Sam was pristine, with tweed slacks in greys and light browns and pressed shirts to coordinate. But currently, he seemed to have worn yesterday's attire that was missing a cufflink, wrinkly and untucked. His grey hair was unkempt, and he could have done with a good twenty-four hours of sleep, in my opinion. It was surprising to see him shopping in such a state, but I would bask in it, nonetheless.

"Are you incapable of watching where your own cart is going?" I was in no mood for his rude tone. "I didn't realize I was in the presence of royalty. My apologies, King Sam. I won't make that mistake again."

"Young lady, it's called common courtesy." His light posh accent made every word sound like a scolding. Too bad Tanner lacked the lure of a good accent. Would have made him less repulsive. "That is no way to speak to an elder. Leave it to Tona to raise you with no values."

"Don't you dare say that name. You have no right to even think about her." I gave him a look of disgust. "I know all about you and Aunt Tona."

"From the sound of it, you know little."

"Don't play coy with me. I saw the letter with the flowers."

The thought of them together still made me sick to my stomach. Why had Aunt Tona never told me? For that matter, why had she not shared about any of the men around town she had seen? How many of the old men that came into the café were actually just there to see her? Had she made me the main barista to avoid ex-lovers?

"I have no idea what you mean," Sam said. "What flowers?"

"The flowers you sent to the café." I pushed my cart to the side, so a mother with a young child whining in the cart could get by.

"I never sent Tona flowers. Well . . ."

"Well, what? You might as well just come clean with it already."

"It's none of your business, young lady."

"What's going on, Papa?" Tanner turned out of the aisle behind Sam and stood beside him. His presence sent a fresh wave of anger through me. He always looked too smug for his own good.

I barely glanced at him, not wanting to give him the satisfaction of acknowledging his presence. He stood a head taller than me, with dark brown hair that looked purposefully styled to appear messy. As usual, his face was lightly shaven, so his dark stubble wrapped from ear to ear, with a mustache to match.

If he did not insist on wearing nerd glasses, I could almost say he was attractive in a prep kind of way. Though the mere idea made me want to hurl. He dressed much like Sam: heather-grey slacks, with a black button-up long sleeve dress shirt. Though the sleeves were casually rolled to his elbows. Was the tea house clientele as stuffy as these two? None of my customers dressed up this consistently. Even the business-owning ones were more casual-business.

"Young Hailey here was just accusing me of sending flowers to Tona."

"Accusing? Did you get your sheriff friend to make sending flowers a crime in this town?" Tanner said with a smirk, asking for my fist. "Shouldn't you be mourning, not stirring up trouble?"

"I'm not stirring anything, Tanner." I gave him a resting face I knew would only egg him on.

"Yeah? Doesn't sound like you at all," Tanner said as he stepped forward. "The other day, I had an outta-towner come in angrier than a wild hog. Told me a story about asking for directions and being sent to a field. You wouldn't happen to know about that, would you?"

"You're blaming me for your customer's inability to follow simple directions? Seems like you need to blame yourself for not having your address listed properly."

Tanner and I had been enemies ever since the day Aubrey punched him. I think his male ego had never forgotten that two little girls almost beat him up. Not that we had much of a chance of being friends anyway with Tona and Sam's history.

"I saw the letter you wrote her in high school," I told Sam. "Did you try to rekindle an old flame? Or maybe you found out she was dating another man and became jealous?"

"Now, just wait a minute, I don't know where you're trying to go with this, but we're done here," Tanner said. "You can't go around digging into my papa's personal business. Tona's dead. It doesn't make a lick of sense to even be digging into their past. What's done is done."

"Hailey, you should be ashamed of yourself." Sam stepped in front of Tanner. "It's none of your business. I will teach you a lesson Tona should have years ago. Don't stick your nose where it doesn't belong."

He stormed off as fast as his legs would carry him, leaving his cart behind with Tanner.

"Great, now you hurt the old man's feelings," Tanner said, grabbing the cart. "He's right. You should be ashamed of yourself."

"Only ashamed that I haven't been clear with everyone else about how toxic your family truly is!"

Maybe I was out of line, but I did not care in the slightest. Something was up with Sam. I just knew it. He was far too out of sorts for him to just be having an off day.

Thursday, February 20th

The café was locked, and the last customer had left nearly an hour ago. They scheduled the meetings for 7:00 p.m., but of course, some ladies showed up early and some late.

One benefit of having a café for the meeting meant everyone could have a drink, and there was plenty of room to spread out. The dragons were having their own private meeting in the back of the café, near the bathrooms, and they expected us dragon protectors to stay up front behind the roaster.

"We thought about skipping the meeting tonight but decided against it," Tori explained once everyone settled in. "Tona was a wonderful woman, and we all miss her dearly, but we're also thrilled to have you as our newest member."

"Thank you," I muttered.

I did not know what else to say, so I glanced at my feet. There was no need to be anxious, but my stomach was uneasy with anticipation for the night.

"She would have wanted us to celebrate her life and yours," Tori continued. "So instead of our usual meeting, let's get you acquainted with the group and celebrate you becoming a dragon tribe member."

I looked to the back and saw that Azure sat in the middle of the other dragons. It was a sight to see, with the rainbow of colors between the various dragons. Each one looked up at him. He had placed himself atop a table. He really took the whole leader thing a bit far.

"I know you have a ton of questions. We've all been there. We will do our best to fill in where we can. We are Tribe Rune and cover the Texas Hill Country. As Azure has hopefully already begun your lessons, the dragon's natural habitat is the cave systems around the world."

I already knew this, but what I did not know was when Azure and I were to confront her and Butter. The other ladies letting Tori take lead on the introduction struck me as odd with how Azure described her, but for this first meeting, I planned to just let the group take the lead. Not like he gave me any directions to do otherwise.

"Once the humans started exploring the caves, the dragons realized they had to protect their home, so they sent liaisons to keep tabs on the human world. In exchange for us guarding their well-being, they lend us a hand in running a successful business."

"Azure just told me about how he helped Aunt Tona make the coffee."

Tori smiled. "Exactly. It's the same for all of us. I'll let everyone introduce themselves and their area of expertise. Then we can answer questions. If you want, you can start us off and tell us a bit about yourself."

I fought down a laugh. My brain flashed the scene of an AA meeting in my mind. *Hi, I'm Hailey. Hi, Hailey. And I protect a dragon.*

"Um, okay," I stuttered. Why had I not prepared an introduction? Of course, tonight would be get-to-know-you night. "Well, I'm Hailey, and I never know what to say in these things."

Everyone laughed, and it eased my tension a bit.

"While I have been helping Tona in the café for as long as I can remember, I never knew she led a double life. I am excited to get to know all of y'all. My life pretty much revolves around coffee, reading, and food."

After another round of laughter, the lady to my left spoke up.

"I'm Sofia. I live in Burnet and run Mahogany Chic. It's a handmade furniture store. I'm a founding protector, so this year will be fifty years."

Sofia was an older woman. Probably even older than my great-aunt had been. Just like Tona, Sofia had an excellent fashion sense. It made sense that she would run a furniture store.

"My daughter is taking over most of the day-to-day work. I'm sure you'll meet her soon. I'm the guardian of Ash Rune. He creates intricate patterns in the grains of our wood and helps with creating unique forms for our furniture."

She took a sip of her cappuccino.

"Hey Hailey! I'm Beth." She cleared her throat and took a drink of her blended caramel latte. It came with a dash of salt and a mug lined with actual caramel. "I own a biker hot spot in Buchanan Dam called Flamed."

While she had to have been in her late forties, her appearance screamed biker through and through. Leathers, long and dark wavy grey hair, and a gruff captivating voice. Her love for life flowed through her every word.

"It sounds like a rough crowd, but they're teddy bears. Ember's flame-broiled burgers keep them satisfied, anyway. You'll have to come out and try it out for yourself. Best burger in the state, I swear it! We've been in the tribe for, oh, seventeen years probably?"

I did my best to keep track of each of the ladies. But it felt more like I was back in school, and there would be a test at the end of the meeting.

"I'm Elizabeth, but just call me Liz."

She reminded me a lot of my own mother—chestnut shoulder-length straight hair, tall, and probably shopped at stores like the GAP exclusively. Though I had always viewed Aunt Tona as my "chosen" mother.

"Josiah and I live in Llano. We create jewelry and other touristy wares out of clay at Fire 'n Clay Studio. We've been bonded for eleven years."

"It's great to finally meet you, Hailey. I'm Vera. Garth is my companion in the garden. We own Little Sprouts in Granite Shoals."

On the knees of her overalls were two mud stains that looked fresh, and her grey hair was in long pigtails. She had ordered an iced tea but settled for iced coffee when I explained we did not serve tea. Guess she thought I might have changed the tea rule.

"Plants from our nursery grow perfectly no matter your skill," Vera continued. "My granddaughter just moved in with us to help me around the nursery. She's about your age, so I'm excited for

the future of this tribe. Oh! Almost forgot, fifty years for us too. Guess we're the last two, Sofia!"

"I've got that bet in the bag," Sofia said with a chuckle. The room filled with laughter, then quickly silenced into a somber remembrance of the loss of a founding member.

The next lady cleared her throat. "My name is Betty. I live in Horseshoe Bay and own Stitch Therapy."

She looked a little out of place for the area wearing a yoga outfit, with white hair in a tight bun atop her head. It had shocked me a bit since she brought a fast-food joint lemonade in with her.

"You'd think Patchwork would have me out of a business, with as good of a job as he does creating quilts that last, but people keep coming back for our beautiful creations. We've been sewing together for twenty-nine years."

"Hey, Hailey, I'm so glad you're going to be a part of this tribe. I know we had a few classes together in high school, but for posterity's sake, I'm Skylar. I inherited Shadow just three years ago, so you can lean on me for support while you adjust.

"We own Brimstone Beauties, creating lawn ornaments and home wall decor. You're going to love this tribe; they are the family I've always wanted."

I thought I recognized her during Tona's funeral. She was the only other woman my age, and she took my recommendation of a Hemlock Americano—an Americano topped with steamed vanilla milk, and whipped cream. It would be a great help to have someone to talk to about the adjustment.

I adored her natural red hair, though I remember her not being that fond of it or the freckles that came with it. The green and white dress she wore complimented her complexion perfectly.

"You already know all about me, but Butter has been in my care for six years," Tori said. "I know it's a lot to take in at once. Do you have questions we can answer for you?"

I had hundreds of questions. Number one still being, when was Azure going to make his announcement? I kicked myself mentally for not asking him ahead of time.

Tori was the last person I wanted to ask questions to. But with the ladies passively letting her lead, it did not seem like I had a choice. The more I learned about her, the more it seemed that Azure had been right. He would never let me live that down, but at least the murder would be solved.

"What are the dragons talking about?"

"We don't know," Vera said. "They don't share their meetings with us."

"They might be in the same room," Betty said, "but their meetings are always private. I can't recall the last time Patchwork shared a tidbit from a meeting."

"Rightly so," Sofia said. "Azure will tell you anything you have to know. Otherwise, it's best to leave them to their business and us to ours."

I felt like they caught me with my hand in a cookie jar.

Was this how the meetings would be? The more experienced ladies talking down to me?

I looked at Skylar, and her eyes said she knew how I felt. I bet she would get along with Aubrey. We could have a proper girls' night out. At least until 10:00 p.m., when Ziti the Great closed.

There was always Wish You Were Beer, but that was very much a guys' sports bar. Not the ideal location for a girls' night.

"So, what are our meetings usually like then?" I asked.

"Oh," Tori said, "the weekly meetings are really for the dragons. We just get together to discuss any news that comes up and make sure they get home safe."

"And the meetings have always been here at Aconite Café?"

"Yes," Betty said.

"Though it would be nice to change up the location sometimes," Tori said.

"I like the café," Skylar said. "It's roomy."

"Tori." Sofia's stern face made me shudder and make a mental note not to cross her. "Since you need a reminder yet again, the meetings are held in the business that holds the tribe leader, which would never be decided by us."

At that moment, the dragons walked over in a single-file line. Butter sat alone where the circle had been.

"I hereby banish Butter and Victoria from the weekly meetings for one month," Azure transmitted, and from the faces of the other women, I realized he had spoken to everyone at once.

"WHY?" Tori screamed and caught herself. "What did we do?"

"If you continue this childish act of playing dumb, it will be for longer. You know exactly why, as we've already addressed the matter with you," Azure transmitted. "But for the sake of the tribe's knowledge, Tori and Butter conspired to poison me with rosemary."

The ladies all gasped in unison.

"You didn't." Skylar turned to her left to face Tori. "How could you? You know full well—"

"We don't believe she acted with malice," Shadow transmitted.

His thoughts sounded twice as deep as Azure's. The words echoed inside my skull.

Josiah transmitted, "We found that Butter intentionally deceived Tori into adding the rosemary to the treats she served him."

"He was so sick," I said. "There was puke everywhere."

"I didn't realize," Tori said. "You have to believe—"

"Regardless," Azure cut her off, "your hand made the treat and served it. You are the protector of Butter. I realize it has been some time since I punished a tribe member, so everyone take note: Dragons and their protectors are held to the same accountability. I banish you and Butter for a month. At which time, we will discuss if there will be any further actions taken against you. This means none of you are to conduct business with them, and their bakery will be on a one-month hiatus to the public as well. Sorry, Hailey."

At least he apologized, but a little heads-up would have been nice. How in the world was I going to replace her baking? The entire town expected me to carry those fresh treats for their morning coffees.

"You're dismissed," Azure continued. "We need to speak with Victoria and Butter. Alone."

The ladies left their drinks and quickly filed out of the front door. Tori hung her head as everyone left in what I assumed was an effort to avoid eye contact with any of them.

Thursday, February 20th

"We need to address the sloth in the room," I started, knowing full well Azure would be unamused at my antics. But I wanted to lighten the mood a bit, if only for my sake. Not even a smirk from Tori. Tough crowd.

"I'm so sorry," Tori said. "I never meant to poison you."

She turned to Azure. "I swear I didn't know. It was—"

"We're not here to discuss your actions," Azure transmitted. "That matter is closed for now."

"Where were you last Friday night?" I blurted out.

I watched Tori closely, looking for any sign of guilt or deception if she tried to lie. So far, she only displayed complete shock at the change in subject.

"You mean Valentine's?" She looked at her feet. "If you must know, I was at home with Butter."

"It's true," Butter transmitted. "On my honor." He straightened up and flared his wings out as if to pose for a moment.

"We know that's worth its weight in tea leaves," Azure transmitted. "Is there any way to corroborate this?"

"We live alone, as you are aware." Tori fought down tears. "After closing the bakery for the day, we went straight home and didn't leave. Why are you interrogating us? What does it even matter?"

I leaned back in my chair. After the ladies left, I had moved in close to her, and Azure sat right at her feet. But being this close was not comfortable, and I did not want to be within her reach. I would not say I knew Tori well enough to know that angering her would not lead to violence.

"We suspect you may have had a hand in Tona's death," I said.

"What!?" Her face dropped, and her cheeks burned red. "Tona's death was an accident of her own doing."

"What exactly are you trying to say?" Butter transmitted.

"We don't think it was an accident," Azure transmitted. "She was a graceful woman, and there's no way she would have tripped and fallen on her own. Even if she had fallen, the force it would take to cause her death would only come from a greater force than falling. Someone killed her, and we intend to find out who!"

"It wasn't me," Tori said, "and Butter was at home with me all night. So, there's no way he could have done it. It is appalling that you would even blame us."

"At what point are you going to stop lying?" I said. Enough was enough.

She sighed and crossed her arms. Why people had such a hard time with being straightforward and honest, I would never understand. Liars were the scum of society.

"I am not lying. What do you want from me?"

"The truth," I said. I hoped my tone and expression appeared determined, even though I felt out of my league for interrogating suspects.

"You already know the truth. Tona the Magnificent had an accident. Is the police report not enough for you?"

Azure let out a growl at that. Tori and Butter sat up straighter.

"How exactly would they know whether it was an accident or a purposeful shove?" I said.

"Why would we hurt our own tribe member?" Butter transmitted.

"No, the police report is not enough evidence. We suspect foul play, and you two had the most motive," I said.

"Hardly." She seemed to get some of her haughty demeanor back. I hoped that Azure would step in and do a better job of putting her in her place than I was.

"You two have been bonded long enough to know full well what that entails on an emotional level," Azure transmitted. "Butter can attest to what it felt like when Tori and Tona went at it during the meetings. The night Tona was murdered, I felt that same feeling before the bond went cold. The police report is nothing compared to the emotional evidence I have for my claims."

They both sat silent. I could not tell if they were speaking to each other or contemplating their next move. But one way or another, I wanted the truth.

"Stop playing dumb with us," I said. "Y'all were always trying to undermine her and Azure, and you've just poisoned him. You could have killed him."

"Never," Butter transmitted. "Azure may be full of himself and need to be taken down a peg, but killing him is a bit far. I ate one of the treats myself. It made me sick, but it wasn't nearly enough to kill a dragon. I would never—"

"Enough," Azure transmitted, bumping his head against Tori's leg. "It is no secret that you two fought constantly. I saw your order of beans missing from the counter when I got back to the café that night. I know you were here within the hour of her death. Explain yourself."

"Fine. You're right. I was here that night. She thought she was so special, having a Valentine's date. When I came to drop off her pastries order, she was fluttering around on cloud nine about the dinner she had earlier," Tori spat. "And she always held the meetings. It was like she thought she was better than the rest of us."

"She was certainly better than you," Azure transmitted. "Was there anyone else in the café while you were here that night?"

"It was just the two of us," Tori said, hardly trying to control her anger. "Tona was working on filling bags from the roaster and locked the door behind me when I left."

Silence fell between us, and we eyed each other with suspicion as we contemplated what they had said. A loud crash broke the tension in the back of the café.

"What the tea?! Wait here," I said with a start. The conversation had been more tense than I realized.

Azure and I ran to the back door. I looked for a weapon to grab on my way, but all I had was the mop water I had yet to dump.

Before I opened the door, I set the bucket on the washer, just in case. After glancing down at Azure, I opened the door as fast as possible, hoping to startle whoever was still making noise on the other side.

The trash cans were in disarray, and knelt at the dryer vent was Tanner with what looked to be a small crate of rats.

"Tanner Wilcox, what in the tea are you doing at my café!?" I yelled at the top of my lungs. "You have some nerve showing up here like this."

Tanner kicked the vent as he stood up. Azure hissed beside me, letting it flow into a light growl. He was ready to jump on him if Tanner tried anything.

"You're one to tal—"

"Don't you dare try to weasel out of this. It looks like you were *just* about to put rats in my vent! When have I ever been within five feet of your rancid shop?"

He looked me in the eye with his trademark smirk. "Things aren't always as they appear. My family seems to teach you more values than your own lately."

Without a second thought, I slapped him across the face. He stumbled back a few steps, and to my relief, the smirk melted off.

"Let's try again, shall we?" I said with a new drive in confidence. "What are you doing behind my café?"

"How about I say sorry, and we forget the entire thing?" He refused to meet my eyes but also had not fully shaken off the shock of being slapped.

"Sorry for trying or for getting caught?"

"All of it."

"Right, makes sense." I gave him a blank look and crossed my arms. "Chastise me for making accusations this morning, then add weight to them, and ask that I forget it all? I'm going to need a better explanation than that."

"It's no secret that you might sell the café," Tanner said. "I was only trying to make your decision easier."

"Selling? Don't tell me you're running with the gossip mill these days."

"I've spoken to Brett myself. Getting information from the source is hardly considered gossip," he said, clearly starting to get his pompous air back.

I laughed out loud. "Unless the source is being a bit hubris in his conquests."

"Only time will tell, Hailey," he said, smirking again.

"Well then, consider me time, as I am here to tell you I'm not selling. The café has never been up for sale, it will never be up for sale, and Brett Townsend is full of tea if he thinks for a second he will get his hands on this property."

"Tea isn't a cuss word, you know. Maybe you should try it before you knock it."

"It is a vile, disgusting, leech of a drink, just like your entire family. You are as dead as tea leaves to me, Tanner Wilcox. Get out of my sight before I call William and press charges."

He looked like he was going to get smart with me, so without thinking, I grabbed the dirty water beside me and threw it in his face.

"You should pay better attention to the weather before leaving the house," I said.

"You're going to pay for this," he said with a growl that scared me more than I wanted to admit.

"No. I'm not," I said, hoping for the second time that night that my fears were not coming through in my tone. "You come within my line of sight again, and I will get a restraining order against your family. I dare you to test me."

He looked as if he was going to fling a retort at me but then gave up and ran off. I suspected he knew William would not think twice about putting him in a cell. Or maybe losing to a girl again was too much for him to bear?

"Well done," Azure transmitted. "I'm proud of you. That's the first actual sign of spunk I've seen in you since the bonding. Your aunt would be proud."

I picked him up and ran my finger between his eyes, along the ridge of his nose. In the cutesiest tone I could manage, I said, "You're such a cute kitty when you get mad."

"Dragon!" Azure transmitted.

"Cutest kitty in the world."

I kept rubbing his nose the whole way back to where Tori and Butter sat waiting on us. If they thought it odd that I was petting Azure and calling him a kitty, they kept that opinion to themselves.

"Now, where were we?" I asked.

It seemed less likely that they had killed off Aunt Tona. Not that I had ever *really* believed it. Though, Azure sure could be convincing when he wanted to be.

I took my seat, all the while petting Azure. He did not protest the petting. In fact, his purrs grew stronger. He may look like a dragon, but he was all kitty.

"We had nothing to do with your aunt's death," Butter transmitted.

"I swear it," Tori chimed in.

"We believe you," Azure transmitted between purrs. "Though your month-long banishment stands."

"Tori, I will find another vendor. At least for the month."

"I understand."

Not that I had any idea who that new vendor would be.

Would customers notice if the pastries changed to store-bought?

"Before you leave, I want to make it perfectly clear," Azure transmitted, "that this conversation is not to leave this room. If I discover that you have lied about anything you've said tonight, I will be forced to take my findings to the elders."

"Yes, sir," they said in unison.

Tori leaned over and gathered up Butter. Together they left in a hurry, and I swear I heard Tori crying as she shut the door behind her.

I put Azure down and locked the front door.

"That's enough excitement for one night," I said as I shut off the lights.

"Agreed," Azure transmitted.

"That Tanner," I said.

"Your guess about it being Sam is looking more likely."

"You don't say."

Friday, February 21st

"You'll never guess what happened last night," I said first thing as Aubrey walked behind the counter. "Follow me."

I had almost called her after we settled in for the night, but I knew it would only scare her into sending William over.

"This better not be a gimmick to get me to forget to remind you about your appointment with the accountant."

"Tea. You saw right through that one."

"I know you," Aubrey said, scrunching eyebrows together to make her scolding face.

"You only think you know me! The past thirty years have been lies and propaganda." I was laughing so hard I could barely get the words out.

"Yeah, okay. So what's the news? There is news, right?"

"Well, yes," I said. "As you should know by now, I rarely greet people with 'you will never believe this' unless something unbelievable is going on. But it seems like your knowledge of me is fading."

"Ha ha, a real comedian you are." She laughed, then turned as serious as she could. "I'll give you that one." Her tone was skeptical, but her snickers ruined any seriousness she was going for.

I led her to the storeroom. No good would come from having the customers overhear. Not that any of the gossipers were in yet.

But the last thing I wanted was for a town gossip to run around telling everyone I was looking into Tona's murder. At best, it would tip the murderer off and cause them to flee. At worst, they would come after me before I figured out who it was.

"What's up?" she asked.

I could not pin down if she was more curious or excited about what I was going to tell her.

"I need you to keep a secret," I whispered.

Aubrey stepped in close and whispered, "Oh yeah? This feels like a fountain-of-soap-level secret."

"Worse."

Her eyes widened, and she pursed her lips together in anticipation.

"Does worse mean the same thing in your language?"

"Oh, come on already!" she said. "The fountain happened like fifteen years ago! It's about time you've topped it!"

"You're horrible, you know that?"

"It's why you love me," she said with an innocent smile. "Now spill the beans!"

"Probably so. All right, all right."

For ten minutes, I walked her through the past week, though I sidestepped Azure being a dragon. It would be hard enough convincing her that someone murdered Aunt Tona without bringing up the whole reason I believed it. I did not think for a second that she would buy the “my pet cat was, in fact, a dragon, and he said so” line.

"Do I need to remind you already that you can tell no one?" Azure transmitted.

"Get out of my head!" I transmitted, avoiding Aubrey's curious look.

"Close your mind! I'm trying to sleep!"

That kitty was moments away from losing pastries for breakfast. Me not being able to block him out yet was on him. Any time he was ready, he could stop playing games and teach me.

She already knew how obsessed I was with murder mystery books. Making the leap to investigating an accident could not be that far off from believable.

It was a true testament to our friendship that the whole time I explained my week and theories, Aubrey nodded along and did not question the idea once. I do not know if I would have been willing to follow along had she been the one saying it. After all, her husband had been in charge of the investigation and cleared it as an accident.

I guess no one in a small town wants to imagine they have a murderer living amongst them.

"What the tea!" Aubrey said, breaking the whisper silence. "Since when do we keep secrets this big from each other?"

"I *know*," I said. "*I'm sorry*. It all just kind of happened, and it never seemed like the right time to announce it. Forgive me?"

"I don't know. This hurts deep." She laughed and put her finger to her heart. "Right here, you hurt me right here."

"I'll make it up to you! I promise!"

"I'm holding you to that."

We let a comfortable silence fall between us. I still was not sure what to think about everything that had happened. But I hoped that by filling Aubrey in, she could help me narrow the suspect list.

"So, you think it was Sam and Tanner?" Aubrey asked.

"At this point, it's where the evidence points," I said. "Sam could have easily come over here because he wanted to confront her about his feelings. With how Tori claims Tona was acting, he could have discovered her current love interest and pushed her into a fit of jealousy. You know how crazy love can make people."

"That's no lie."

As the wife of the town's sheriff, she heard all the horror stories of couples fighting. But not once had it resulted in murder. *Bloody nose, black eye? Sure. But murder? No. Marble Falls is a peaceful town. At least it was.*

"What are you going to do about it?" Aubrey asked.

"Nothing yet," I said. "I don't have enough evidence. I needed to get it all off my chest, let someone else ponder over it for a while."

"Tanner has some nerve showing up here," she said, deep in thought. "He just took your little drink feud to a Hatfield and McCoy level."

"That's exactly what I told him last night. He's such a pompous tea-tart. I hope he showed up to work with a hand-shaped bruise on his face."

"He better heed your warning. William would be on him so fast for harassing you," Aubrey said. "I would have loved to see his face when you threw that dirty water on him."

"It was an expression I won't soon forget," I said.

We both burst into laughter as the front bells jingled.

"Looks like you're saved by the bell. Time for you to get ready to go."

I stuck my nose in the air and crossed my arms. She laughed at my antics as she walked out to greet the customer.

I knew I would not enjoy a single minute of the meeting with Ben. Numbers were not my cup of joe.

After an hour of going over the accounts and where all the finances stood, I had a foggy brain and was ready for a fresh espresso.

Unfortunately, we were not done.

I did, however, learn that Ben was a neat freak, to a level that I had only witnessed in the movies. When I set my pen down

during the first round of signing, he swept it up before moving on to place it back in the pen holder.

His office did not have a speck of dust in sight—a battle that I continually lost at the café. I would have asked him for his secret, but during one pause, he declined small talk, so I instead stayed silent and admired the landscapes on the wall.

I could not remember the last time I had been in an accounting office, so I had no idea what average décor was for one, but it reminded me of artwork I would find at my dentist. Typical blue skies and fields of wildflowers.

My phone dinged, but I ignored it, trying my best to focus on what Ben was telling me.

After two more dings, I looked down at the screen.

Aubrey: The health inspector is here! Says someone called him about rats. Wonder who that was.

Aubrey: Let him know you were out.

Aubrey: I GOT THIS. STAY UNTIL YOU GET EVERYTHING DONE!

I assumed the color drained from my face as I met Ben's eyes.

"Did you hear—is everything okay?" Ben asked.

"The health inspector is at the café."

"Do you need to go?" he asked.

"No, Aubrey gave me direct orders to stay and finish."

He laughed. "Okay, let's get back to it then."

After a bit of paperwork shuffling, he repeated the sentence I missed.

"You are going to have to call the insurance offices and provide them with the death certificate so they can transfer the policies to your name."

"Okay, I can do that," I said while pretending to make a note in my phone. I needed to finish making a list of all the things I needed to do around the café. Phone calls were last on that list.

"The last thing we need to discuss is who you want to be on the account in case of your untimely death."

I shifted in my seat, not sure how to answer. This seemed like something I needed to discuss with Azure, not an accountant. It would have been helpful if Ben gave me homework instead of springing these questions on me.

"We can change this person at any time, so don't overthink it. It's best to have someone that you trust and would want to see the café and assets go to."

"I don't really have anyone picked out," I said. I spoke slow and was not focused on the direction he was giving. More letting my thoughts wander over all the people I knew. "I don't have any siblings, and Tona just had Mom . . . I could list Aubrey, but with her being my age, that seems inappropriate. What is she going to do with the café if I die a few years before her . . ."

Ben let me ramble through the people I knew without interrupting me. I doubted Tona had this much trouble deciding it would be me. I had been at the bar stool since I could walk. Coffee was my life. Was there anyone I knew that sat where I sat? Madison. That could work!

"What about Aubrey's daughter, Madison? What would happen if I left it to her and died before she turned of age to inherit?"

"There's an idea," Ben said. He gave me a slight smile. "The café would stay in her name, but her parents would take over the books until she turned eighteen."

"There is no one I trust more than the Brooks family. Let's put Madison. If Aubrey doesn't like it, I can keep thinking and get back to you."

Truthfully, I knew Aubrey would love it, but it was Azure I needed to approve the choice with. Yet another reason he would use as to why I should have just brought him. When he was right, he was right.

"Sounds good," Ben said and typed a few more lines on his computer before his printer came to life.

I fidgeted as I waited for him to compile the next stack of papers for me to sign. Would the café pass inspection? Why was he even there? I could not recall the last inspection we had outside of the required ones.

Maybe that was what Tanner meant when he said that time would tell. Did he know about this? If Brett put him up to the rats, what if it was so he could call the inspector on us? Maybe Brett didn't know that Tanner had failed. Or called ahead of time so whether or not it happened, we would still get inspected. The café was clean. There was no reason for this insane line of thought. We'd pass. Ben was waiting on me to get out of my thoughts again.

"It will be okay. Y'all will pass," he said. "I just need you to sign in a few places."

I took the pen from the holder and signed in the designated areas as he pointed them out. Great, now all that has to happen is for me to die. Woo.

"I'll get these to Vivian," he said as he put a stack of papers into a manilla folder. "Tona usually came in biweekly to discuss the accounts and go over the hard numbers. So if you want to continue that, we can set the Friday of every other week as our scheduled meeting?"

"Okay, that sounds good," I said. "Keeping this time?"

"Yes, that will work for me," he said. "Unless you have any questions for me, you are all set."

"Great!"

"Wasn't too painful, was it?" he asked, looking up from the paperwork he was finalizing and putting away.

He was back to the pristine showroom office just like that.

"Not as bad as my nightmares were leading me to believe." I gave him a wink, stood, and shook his hand. "See you in two weeks."

Even though I was mere blocks away from the café, it felt like the longest walk imaginable.

Friday, February 21st

I walked in the café's backdoor a bit more apprehensive than I should have been. I knew full well there was no cause for concern. But nonetheless, I was nervous about the results.

I snuck to the door that separated the storeroom from the café and put my ear to the door. The normal café bustle made it hard to hear for the inspector, so I cracked the door a bit.

Aubrey and a man were speaking in hushed tones as they had their sights on the under-counter area. To my surprise, she did not look nervous at all.

Man, I love her.

Since she had everything under control, I decided to follow the plan I made on the way over and slowly closed the door.

"Why are you sneaking?" Azure transmitted.

I turned to discover he had snuck up behind me as I attempted to eavesdrop on Aubrey.

"I am not sneaking. I just did not want to disturb them," I transmitted as we walked upstairs to the apartment.

"Okay, that's believable," Azure transmitted. I could sense his eye roll in my mind. "When can you be bothered to feed me?"

Everything always came back to food with him. I sent an eye roll of my own.

"I need to make a few phone calls," I transmitted. "They won't even know I am back yet."

"Who are you hiding from? Did the accountant go that badly?" he transmitted.

I followed him to his food bowl and opened a can of seafood-flavored wet meat. Yuck. The smell of these cans would be the death of my nose. Seafood was my least favorite food.

"I am not hiding. It went fine. I just want to be prepared before I face the health inspector."

"Health inspector?" Azure stopped eating to make eye contact with me. "That explains why Aubrey was showing someone around the storeroom. Thought she was trying to sell the place out from under you."

"Why on earth . . . nope, don't answer that. I don't want to know." I sat down on the couch, stretching my legs out.

"Lesson number ten: Never let your guard down," he transmitted.

"Right. Anyway, the health inspector is here looking for rats," I transmitted.

He finished eating and went to stretch out on the couch, barely glancing at me. "Don't look at me. I kill any rats I see."

"I know," I transmitted. "This is Tanner."

I picked up the phone next to me but stopped mid-dial. Tanner was too stupid to plan out a thing like this. He had mentioned wanting me to sell. Also, Tanner knew he failed. Why would he still report us to the health inspector?

I went over all of this a million times since Aubrey's text. Why was I second-guessing myself still? Ever since Tona's death, I was questioning too many of my own choices. I needed to get back to my roots and let logic lead me.

"Are you saying you aren't always this scatterbrained?" Azure transmitted. "That's a relief."

I rolled my eyes. Snark was not worth my time in responding to. I needed to focus on the real issue. Who should I call first, Brett or Tanner?

"Fine. Don't acknowledge my wit. Tanner could have reported it before attempting to put them in the vent."

"What if Brett put him up to it?" I transmitted.

If that guy was sleazy enough to gloat about sales not even in discussion yet, what else was he capable of? Maybe that was how he became real estate agent of the year for the Highland Lakes area.

"Makes sense. He has the motive to sabotage businesses into selling," Azure transmitted. "There are many properties around town that are family-owned but would make for a great asset to any real estate company. This building included."

"I guess I should call him first then, see what he has to say."

I started to dial Brett's number when Azure head-butted my arm.

"Not yet," he transmitted. "Tell me what happened at the accountant before you get all discombobulated by those tea-tarts."

"Really? Like that is important right now?!"

"I, for one, think my future is extremely important. Now, please enlighten me."

"Oh fine." I slammed the phone on the receiver. "What do you want to know?"

"Are you hard of hearing?" Azure's growl reverberated through my mind.

"Can you speak to me without attitude?" I said aloud, crossing my arms.

"Fine." His tone changed to a lighter one that was clearly fake. The accent did nothing to hide the snide feelings behind it. "What choices did you make at the accountant?"

"Oh, right," I said, easing my shoulders a bit. "I was hoping to have time to think through all of that before talking to you about it."

"Why? Don't you think I have a right to be in the decision-making? We are partners in this café, you know."

He hopped off the couch and shook out his wings.

"Valid. I don't know. I'm still getting used to all of this. It caught me off guard at the accountant's office when he asked me to name an heir."

"So, did you tell him you'd get back to him?"

"Not exactly," I said.

"What does that mean? I guess it's not like you have many options," Azure transmitted, pacing the room.

"What is that supposed to mean?"

"Exactly what it sounds like. Who do you have to pass down to?"

"I took care in thinking through everyone I know and asked Ben many questions to help make a decision on this matter."

"Too bad you didn't ask the person who matters most in the decision," Azure transmitted in a mumble.

"If you can't trust me to pick a suitable heir, then why are we even bonding? Trust goes both ways, and you have yet to teach me a thing about being a protector or giving me an inch of trust."

"All right, all right. You've made your point. Who did you choose?" He sat down near the foot of the couch.

"After thinking through all the possibilities, I decided it would be best if I picked someone that was currently a child as it would give ample time to evaluate them and indoctrinate them into the life of coffee. As you know, I don't know many children or people in general, but there is one family that I trust with my life."

"Out with it already!"

"I chose Aubrey's daughter, Madison."

"I see," he transmitted.

I knew no matter who I chose, he would not be okay with it. But I had not expected him to be so hostile about the decision. It was not like I was going to die tomorrow. We had time to get it right.

"Ben, let me know that I can change this person at any time. But with how excited Madison is about the café, I don't think it will be necessary."

"She is what, five at most? How can you know that?"

"Six. She turned six this year," I said, standing up to pace the room. "It's called intuition. You know, a gut feeling. Don't dragons get those?"

"Yes, we have gut feelings. Though I can't say I had one with you."

"Rude! Stop being like this! Who would you have had me pick?"

He sat quietly, only moving his eyes to watch me pace the apartment.

There was no point in this conversation. I made the best choice out of the people I had to pick from. But truth be told, even if I had a large circle of friends and family to decide from, I would still have gone with Madison. Aubrey was a sister to me. If I died, there was no one out there that would have the café's best interests at heart than her. She would be phenomenal at helping Madison run the café. She was proving my point as we spoke, with how she took control of the health inspector's surprise visit.

"All right, you win," Azure sighed and hopped back onto the couch. I followed him there, hoping this change in demeanor was him admitting defeat.

"You have to understand. It took me months to choose Tona. Even in the first few years of us bonding, I was not sure I made the right choice. After fifty years with her, it is extremely hard for me to turn over such a large decision to someone I barely know. I don't even know if you will be suitable yet."

"You know what, I get that. I really do. Trust issues suck. But life has to go on. Decisions have to be made. We have to trust the people thrown into our lives whether or not we are ready to."

I pause to wipe tears from my eyes. I might have been getting a bit too worked up over the situation, but if we were supposed to be spending the rest of my life together, then we needed to come to an understanding.

"When Ben threw that curveball at me today, I didn't take it lightly," I said, petting him behind the horn. "While I felt I needed to give him an answer right then, I knew the weight my choice held in the lives of the people I care for. That includes you."

"I'm sorry," Azure transmitted in a whisper.

"What was that?" I said, thinking I misheard him.

"I'm sorry!" he transmitted louder. "I let my own grief and fears impede in a moment that I should have known wasn't easy for you either. For that, I am sorry."

"I accept your apology."

We sat in silence for a while, and I hoped that he, too, was using the time to think over our predicament. We were either going to come to an understanding, or there would be many miserable years ahead of us. What even happened when a protector and dragon did not get along?

"Within the dragon code," Azure transmitted in a calm, steady voice, "it is written that dragons must find a way to work out any difficulty between protector and dragon. As with the transferring of bonds, inevitably, a pairing will not pan out for one reason or another. In the unfortunate situation where there is no way to come to an understanding, an elder will come to the surface and wipe the knowledge of us from the protector's memory."

"What? How do they live? What if they have nothing but the business left to them? That seems so extreme!"

"Calm down. It is not a choice that is made lightly or without all parties involved having a say. I can't even recall the last time it happened. But the protector and their tribe work out an agreement. They help her find a job and set her up financially.

Plus, they work out the memories for the elder to implant in place of the ones they are losing."

I sat speechless, staring at him with wide eyes. Starting over with false memories had to be one of the worst experiences a person could go through. There was no way they would not always be suspicious of the gaps that would inevitably appear. To get to where I could not stand the sight of Azure, that much was unimaginable.

"Like I said, it is a last-resort clause," he transmitted. "While rarely used, it is important to prepare for all situations that could arise from bonding with humans."

"I get it. I am just . . . wow."

"I may be hard on you at times and not always the easiest to communicate with—"

"That's the understatement of the week," I interrupted.

He shot me a look and continued without a retort. "But I know in my gut we will do great things together. I will stand behind your pick for an heir."

I gave him a light smile. That was one of us, at least.

"I trusted Tona more than I have ever trusted anyone in my entire life. She chose you for a reason. Don't for a second think you were a last-resort choice or picked because you were her only option. You have what it takes to be a great tribe leader. We just need to beat it out of you."

He chuckled with the last line, and I let out a breath of relief. If Tona believed in me, then I would give her the benefit of the doubt. I could master being a protector, just like I had mastered any other challenge thrown at me, though it would have been better if she was still with us. She would know exactly how to handle the health inspector and the sabotage. Tanner or Brett, who to call first.

In my heart, I knew who the mastermind was of trying to get me to sell the café. And if he thought for a second that any amount of money or sabotage would get me to sell, he had another thing coming.

I can do this.

With Azure's light snores filling my mind, I picked the receiver back up and dialed.

Friday, February 21st

"Lake Front Real Estate, Brett speaking."

"Brett, it's Hailey."

"Oh, um, hi Hailey." His voice cracked.

"Do you have a minute?"

"Sure. Were you able to find Tona's paperwork?"

Someone's tune had changed. Maybe he was expecting me to accuse him of something.

"No, not yet. Still going through her desk. She held onto just about every paper she touched. So if it exists, it's here."

I still was not sure if I should call him on the gossip surrounding the sale of the café. At the end of the day, he needed to know it was not for sale. But was that an over-the-phone conversation?

"Oh, okay," he said. I could hear the confusion in his voice. Guess he still did not understand why I was calling him.

"Funny thing happened last night," I said, then paused to let him stew in anticipation for a few seconds. "When I was closing up, I ran into Tanner outside the back of the café."

"Tanner?"

"Yes, Tanner Wilcox. He seemed to be under the impression that we'd already closed the deal on the café. Thought it was strange, so I wanted to touch base with you."

"That is strange. I can't remember the last time I was in the teahouse. More of a coffee person myself."

"Right, that's what I thought. I guess you wouldn't know why the health inspector came in this morning with reports of rats either?"

"Inspector?" he asked.

"Yes, the health inspector. Looking for rats."

Was he just going to repeat everything I told him? This man was infuriating.

"Hailey, I don't have a clue what you're talking about."

How fascinating. Somehow I was not buying his act of innocence.

"Just to be clear, you're saying you didn't send Tanner here to put rats in my vent and notify a health inspector?"

"I want to buy the café, that's true. But I never told Tanner to put rats in your building. Did he say I did?"

"When I confronted him last night, he alluded to the fact that his presence involved you."

"I see," he said. "Well, if there isn't anything else you'd like to accuse me of, I need to get back to work. Good afternoon."

The phone clicked, and then the dial tone hummed in my ear. I set it back on the receiver to think.

Guess it would have to be an in-person conversation then. Maybe I should send him a certified letter instead to get the point completely across.

If Brett did not tell Tanner to do it, then it must have been Sam and Tanner. A two-man conspiracy, instead of three. My gut told me Brett had been the mastermind behind it, but maybe I was wrong.

"Wouldn't be the first time," Azure chimed into my thoughts.

"No one asked for commentary from the coffee-bean gallery," I transmitted in a flat tone.

What would they get from the café closing? Revenge? It is not like coffee drinkers switch to tea overnight just because a café closes. They would just change cafés. Once a coffee addict, always a coffee addict.

Brett seemed genuinely calm and surprised at the accusation. But it was hard to say since real estate agents were often well versed in having a perfectly calm demeanor. It would be impossible to sell tough properties without being able to believably pass off a few white lies.

It could not hurt to confront Tanner as well. The worst he could do was hang up on me. I would at least be able to catch him by surprise. After our encounter last night, I was probably the last person he expected a phone call from.

I pulled the phone book out of the drawer and flipped through it to find the number to the tea house. No way was I going to try the number Tona had listed in her little black book. How awkward would that be? "Hey Sam, I know we had it out the other day, and I'm sure you've heard about the other night already, but could you connect me with your tea of a grandson? Thanks."

I laughed to myself at the absurdity.

"You think too much," Azure transmitted in a yawn.

"You know how to solve that problem," I transmitted.

"Giving you a sleeping pill?"

"Har har. If you don't mind, I'm trying to solve a case," I said in a dry tone.

"The case of the health inspector is the least of our concerns," Azure transmitted.

"I need to start small," I transmitted. "Solve a minor case, then work my way up to murder."

Azure chuckled in my mind. "Because we have time for all of this. Unless you're thinking they are connected?"

"Oh right, because when people murder, they usually set their next crime as a lower misdemeanor."

"If you have an obsession with serial killers, please tell me now," Azure transmitted.

"Left field," I said.

"How else would you know what a killer would do?"

"Touché," I said. "Is it okay with you if I make this call now?"

"By all means, investigate why the health inspector is here. For all you know, they never called him. Just doing a surprise inspection."

"Aubrey said he was here because someone saw a rat."

"If only we could find a rat in the sea of secrets that are surrounding us. Call away."

"Thank you, Your Highness," I said and bowed my head to him.

His laugh calmed my nerves. Hopefully, the call would answer some of my questions. Otherwise, I doubted it was worth talking to the enemy.

The phone rang twice, then an older man answered it. "Sereni-tea Tea House, how may we be of service?"

"Good afternoon. Is Tanner available?" I tried my best to disguise my voice, as I did not want him to know it was me before I could get Tanner on the phone.

I could hear the old man fumbling as he went to look for Tanner. Having never actually been inside their shop, I was not sure if they too had a living area upstairs.

"This is Tanner."

"I spoke to Brett." I let the accusation hang on the line. Maybe he would let something slip?

"And?" Tanner asked after he realized I was not going to continue. I hoped it also took him a few seconds to realize who was on the phone.

"Where were you last Friday night?" I blurted.

Okay, maybe sticking to the plan was not in the cards for me. The accusation just slipped out. There could be something to the health inspector case and the murder case being committed by the same person, right?

"No," Azure transmitted.

"Sh!" I transmitted.

"Um, on a date," he said, with a venomous amount of hate. "Let me guess, you were home alone?"

What a jerk. Someone needed to take him down.

"So, you picked her up after you closed up shop?"

"No, I left early," Tanner said. "What business is it of yours?"

"After talking to Brett, I felt it best to put together a timeline."

"Timeline?" Tanner paused. "I don't know what Brett said . . ."

"So, it's only a coincidence that you both want the café to fail? Fascinating."

"It's clear you didn't pay attention to Papa's lesson yesterday regarding keeping your nose in your own business, so I will let you in on some facts."

"Please, bestow your great wisdom upon me, Tanner," I deadpanned him, hoping it would go over his head.

"It will be my pleasure, Hailey," he said without missing a beat. "I may have stooped to your level last night. But your behavior to my papa was uncalled for, and I just snapped. There is no conspiracy. Brett didn't guide me in the ways of sabotage. I just wanted to give you another reason to sell."

"And the health inspector?"

"Umm . . ." He cleared his throat but stayed silent.

"Sorry, must have forgotten to mention that he's here now. Should I send him your way when he finishes up?"

"Like I said. You were out of line. Any fallout from your actions is on you. Don't be disrespectful, and your business won't have to suffer for it."

"Excuse me?" I asked. Who did this guy think he was? Sam was just as guilty as I was if we were talking about respect.

"I mean, he's an old man, and he's been crazy depressed ever since your aunt passed. I don't know how much you actually know about their history, but he loved your aunt. They fought, but I think deep down she loved him too."

An obnoxious laugh escaped me. I could not contain it. This was just too much. The "if he is mean to you, it just means he likes you" defense was obnoxious.

Fighting has never, and will never, equate to a secret crush. What was wrong with these people? Just like my mother, so out of touch with reality. You cannot just explain away a lack of feelings by saying the person is hiding them.

"Somehow, I highly doubt that. Just because every country song seems to think pining and obsessing over the one that said no is acceptable doesn't make it a fact," I said, not betraying my thoughts. "It makes it a mental health issue that you should probably get Sam help for."

"Either way, he has been bent out of shape over the grocery store incident. He just wants to grieve in peace."

"So, you try to ruin her legacy by getting the café shut down?"

"For Pete's sake, Hailey. It was a little sabotage, not murder!"

I laughed again, despite wanting to keep a handle on my emotions. He was just too much. I did not believe a word he said. Tanner was a spoiled brat who only cared about himself. If Brett did not know about the rats, Tanner could have been the one behind it all. He was twisted enough.

Sam was still the most likely suspect, though. If he was so heartbroken over Tona's death, it was more likely because he was guilty about what he had done. If Tanner knew about Sam's undying love for her, then it had to be strong enough to fuel jealousy.

"You know you're still on the phone, right?" Azure transmitted.

Tea.

"I'll let the health inspector know a customer mentioned seeing roaches in your establishment. Have a wonderful day," I said, and hung up.

If I had kept talking, I would have let my true thoughts slip and given them a chance to flee. I had to be missing something.

Was it possible that Tona just had a fluke accident? Tori had said she was lost in the bliss of her date that night.

"Do you realize the accident she would have had to have to cause herself to hit the roaster with enough force to kill her?" Azure transmitted.

"Yes, you've mentioned it."

"Then why do we keep circling back to it?"

"Until we get a confession out of someone, there is no reason to rule out the idea that it was truly a freak accident."

"If you say so," Azure transmitted and yawned again.

"Am I interrupting your nap?"

"Yes. Are you ever going to go down there and relieve Aubrey?"

I looked at the clock. Oops! I probably should have texted her to let her know I was back. It was already after three. No doubt she called William to get the kids. But I did not want to take advantage of her kindness.

I took a deep breath. The health inspector would not tell me anything I did not already know. Might as well get it out of the way. Hopefully, the café passed with flying colors.

"Stop freaking out about it. The café is clean. You clean all the time. Everything will be fine," Azure transmitted.

"I am submitting an official request to be taught how to block you out of my mind. I expect formal training to happen within twenty-four hours."

"Your request has been reviewed and denied. I would miss out on all this free entertainment."

I stuck my tongue out at him and headed downstairs.

Friday. February 21st

Truth be told, I was mildly surprised at how long the inspector stayed. Part of me was expecting him to be gone when I stepped into the storeroom. But that was probably wishful thinking with how my week had gone so far.

He was a thin man in his mid-thirties, wearing khakis and a company polo. Definitely the inspector.

"Hello, Ms. Morton," he said.

Oh no.

Not once in my life had a conversation gone well when it started with Ms. Morton. I looked at Aubrey, memories of the principal's office flooding my mind.

"My name is Mike, and I've had the pleasure of inspecting your café today." He reached out to shake my hand.

"Good afternoon Mike, how'd we do?" I said, a bit apprehensive. He did say pleasure? So it could not be that bad.

"I'm pleased to inform you that Aconite Café passed with flying colors." He handed me the top sheet from his clipboard, which had a score of ninety-three for the café. "Though I must remind you that you're not cleared to have pets in the café."

I looked down and realized that the little fluffball had followed me downstairs. Great timing, Azure.

"Azure doesn't go in the café," I lied. Not the time to deal with that can of worms.

"Very well. I noted that the storeroom door stayed closed for the entire time I was here," he said and looked at Aubrey. "Thank you for your assistance today, Mrs. Brooks."

"You're welcome. Have a safe drive back to Austin," Aubrey said with a genuine smile.

We followed him to the front, so I could lock up after he left.

"So?" Aubrey and I asked simultaneously once I locked the door.

"Jinx," we both said again.

"Double jinx!" we both chimed while laughing.

I walked back behind the counter and brewed myself a blended latte. "Do you want one?"

"Oh no, it's too late for me to be still drinking coffee," Aubrey said. She started in on wiping down the tables and lifting the chairs.

"Whatever, weakling, it's always the right time for coffee," I said with a laugh. After I took my first sip, I let out an enormous sigh of relief. This was exactly what I needed.

"Stop holding out on me. You've had your coffee, now tell me what happened at the accountant."

"You're one to talk! Why did he stay so long? Did he have any comments about the café?"

"Boring," she said. "You're the one that left me here to fend off accusations of rats! You go first!"

"Oh, all right," I said. I gave her a wink. "I could have come home from the accountant early, you know."

"Nope. Not a chance. That was way more important than what was happening here."

"Yeah, it ended up being pretty important. Thanks for covering. I assume William got the kids?"

"It was no problem at all," she said. "He picked them up without complaint. What time did you get home? I didn't hear you climb the stairs."

"I've been home for a few hours. I was going to come into the café, but you had it under control, so I went and made some phone calls instead . . ." I gave her a sly smile to see if she would pick up on the gossip I was holding.

"Oh really? Phone calls to who?" she asked.

"Tanner and Brett," I said. I took another sip of my coffee, purposefully not wanting to make eye contact with her. There was a pause in the noise of lifting the chairs.

I glanced at her, and she was standing with her hand on her hip.

"You are holding out on me again? I thought we talked about this?" she said with mock shock.

"Well, let's just say I have a lot of news. Which do you want to hear about first, the accountant or the boys?"

"I can't imagine the accountant being that interesting, so I guess let's go with the boys first."

By the look on her face, I bet the wait for my gossip was killing her inside. Little did she know, the accounting news would be the more exciting announcement.

"All right, if you're sure, we can chat about them first." I laughed.

"What's that supposed to mean?" She laughed and started back in on lifting the chairs and wiping down the tables.

"Tanner claims Sam loved Tona and that the feeling was mutual!" I said, ignoring her statement. She could stew on what it meant for a bit.

Aubrey mouthed "wow" as I continued, "He also said the rats were payback for the market debacle. Brett acted as if he knew nothing about the whole mess. I don't know who to believe."

"Sam and Tona, really?"

"I know, right?" I rolled my eyes. "Makes me want to vomit."

"I can't imagine Tona hating him as much as she did. And having secret feelings for him?" Aubrey asked, looking toward the ceiling.

"Exactly," I said. "More sounds like Sam was living in a fantasy world to deal with the rejection."

Aubrey broke out laughing.

"The entire conversation was pointless. He pretty much told me it was my fault for him sabotaging us, and Tona's fault that Sam was sad."

"Well, that's obnoxious . . . to say the least." Aubrey shook her head. "Do you think any of them could have killed her?"

"After talking to them, I'm more confused about Tona's death than before I started looking into it. Sam is really the only one with a motive. If he really loved her that much, he could have done it in a jealous rage. But he is an old man. Could he really have the strength to push her hard enough?"

"Good point. Guess it could have really just been an accident." She paused as if pondering over the situation. "So, Brett had nothing to do with the rats?"

"He was pretty adamant that he knew nothing. But I don't know if I buy it," I said, taking another long drink. Blended lattes were stress killers. "I think I am going to mail him a certified letter, letting him know I don't want to sell and officially asking him to drop it."

"That's a good idea. He won't be able to misinterpret that or argue with it."

"Exactly. So how did the inspection go?"

"Honestly, it went great. Mike was thorough and explained everything he was looking for, so I'll be able to add it to the handbook."

I let out a squeal. "That's fantastic! I knew there was a reason I kept you around."

"Oh yeah? We're just friends for my organizing skills, eh?"

"Pretty much." I scrunched my nose at her, and she gave it right back to me. "Is that why it took so long?"

"No, he brought a pest inspector as well to verify there were no signs of an infestation. They inspected the outside of the building too. He said everything was in great condition. They both gave me the impression that they were slightly annoyed to be doing a

surprise inspection because of a complaint that didn't have any proof supporting it."

"I wonder how often they get fake calls," I said.

"No kidding. Seems like they would vet them first before sending people out from Austin."

We let the elevator music fill the silence. Such a waste of a visit.

"So, what happened with the accountant?" she asked as she moved behind the bar to clean.

"Oh! Yes!" I said with a bit more excitement than she was ready for. I cleared my throat to tone it down a bit before continuing. "Overall, it was boring. I signed a ton of paperwork, and he is taking care of giving the lawyer her copies. All I have left to do is call the insurance companies."

"Nice. Not bad for a few boring hours. So what's the excitement for?"

"Well, part of the paperwork required me to pick an heir. I was going to pick you, but I know how much you hate the café, and we're going to be old and grey together so you wouldn't be able to run the café if we die on the same day."

During my rambling, she stopped cleaning to give me an overdramatic shocked expression.

"So then I had to run through all the people I knew that were younger than us and would be able to take over in the event of my death, and I hope you're okay with it because I listed Madison."

"Oh, Hailey," she said, her voice choked, and she rushed around the bar. "Of course, that's okay. I mean, you're as much a part of my family as my own siblings."

She gave me a deep hug, relieving the rest of the tension built up from the day.

"Thank goodness, I was so nervous. Ben said I could change it at any time. But honestly, I can't imagine the café being in better hands than your family."

She wiped her eyes. "You are too kind. I'm going to cry. I know you're not interested in having kids of your own, but I hope you know mine adore you."

"Being an aunt is the best," I laughed. "All the spoils, none of the hassle."

She laughed and walked back around the bar.

"You don't have to clean, you know. I should work a little bit today," I said.

I put my coffee down and went to the windows to wash them.

"Nonsense," Aubrey said. "I've loved working here this week."

"Enough that you might want to stay on?"

She gave me another surprised glance. Her eyes were still glistening. Today made me realize just how much I needed her to be my partner. Even though I knew I would find a new normal at the café without Tona, there was no reason to try to hack it alone. The best jobs were those worked with people that brought us joy.

"I'd have to speak with Will first."

"I figured." I swept up around the tables. "Just something to think about."

She smiled and went back to taking inventory.

"We're down to the last inch of beans," Aubrey reminded me.

"Wish me luck. I'm going to *roast* my first batch tonight."

"Little did she know, it would be the last batch as it would chase all the customers away." She barely got out the last words as she crumpled into a fit of laughter.

"No trust. Friends for all these years, and no trust."

"I am probably the only person who can say I've eaten your cooking before . . . well, tried to anyway."

"Shots fired!" I said. "Roasting is not cooking."

I glanced at Azure to make sure he knew that meant he would have to stick around. He was already relaxing in the windowsill beside it, awaking at Aubrey's departure.

While Aubrey cleaned around the espresso machine, I made my way over to the roaster to clean it for use. I swept underneath and then gathered a rag from the back to wipe out the inside. I at least knew that it needed to be as clean as possible to get the best roast.

"Make sure to wipe the entire basin down well," Azure transmitted. "Beans can get caught under the blades and affect the next batch."

"You could do more than just sit there," I transmitted back.

"Oh? And have her see I'm more than a cat?" he transmitted, and let out a meow to drive home the point.

"Aubrey isn't a viable excuse for your laziness. You'd still be sunbathing if we were alone."

"Touché."

I wiped along the inside of the basin in a systematic pattern to not miss a spot. The closer I got to the center, the dustier it became. I tried to spin the blades, but they did not budge.

"Does the machine have to be on for these to turn?" I transmitted.

"No, they should turn freely. Might be beans."

I ran my finger around the base of the blades and pulled out a golden sleeve cuff.

"Not usually where I store my cufflinks," Azure transmitted, thinking himself clever.

After wiping it off with my rag, I froze. In that moment, I realized who the killer was. It was as if I could see the whole night play out before my eyes.

I kicked over the broom as I turned to run out of the store.

"What's going on?" Aubrey asked.

"I know who did it," I yelled as I unlocked the front door and ran out of the café.

"Wait," Azure transmitted, but I blocked him from my mind.

I was almost positive that Aubrey yelled from the café door, but I was in too much of a panic to think clear enough to hear her words.

Nothing would stop me from getting justice for Tona.

Friday, February 21st

As I jogged the block down Main Street, the black antique streetlamps turned on, bathing the street in a beautiful sea of yellow light. Most everyone had deserted the sidewalks for dinner, but I tried to keep my panic under control to not cause the tourists any alarm.

The last thing I needed was for someone to stop me and ask if I was in danger or needed help.

Stay calm, stay focused. I repeated it to myself as I hurried along the sidewalk.

I took in the scenery to clear my mind. Lake Marble Falls was down the hill, and the hawks circled overhead as they searched for a snack. If I had not been about to confront my aunt's killer, I would have taken a moment to appreciate the view only Marble Falls offered. Life here was a vacation—I never wanted to leave.

One of Tona's favorite parts of living in the Hill Country was the frequent cloudless skies. A person had not experienced a sunset properly until they took in one without a cloud or high rise in sight. The fact that it was one of those miraculous skies as I jogged let me know Tona was with me.

She would never truly be gone. As long as I honored her memory, she would always live on through the people that loved her.

The oranges fading into pinks, purples, then blues warmed my heart and gave me the calm I knew I needed to get this over with. I stopped in front of the door and took a deep breath.

The open sign was off, so I glanced at my watch, tea, past closing time. I peeked through the front window and could see light coming from the back hall. Fingers crossed, I went ahead and tried the front door, anyway. It was unlocked. Thank the beans! Now to see if the right person was working late.

"Hello?" a male voice called from the back as I entered the building. By his questioning tone, he was not expecting a visitor. Guess it would be the last time he left the door unlocked after hours.

I walked into a back office to find him sitting behind a laptop—papers haphazardly spread across his desk.

"You look like you ran here. Did you find the offer?" Brett began to stand, but I held my hand up to stop him.

"Offer? Are you serious right now? You know there was never any offer!"

My heart felt like it was going to pound out of my chest. His face displayed the shock of being caught off guard by my accusation.

"I don't—"

"Don't you dare lie to me!"

My face felt like it was on fire. Every fiber of my being called out for vengeance. I wanted to jump over the desk and strangle him with my bare hands. But I also knew that Aunt Tona would never have wanted that fate for me.

Instead, I held out my fist and opened it to reveal the cufflink.

I let the moment hang in the air, waiting to see if he would admit the truth. But with no such luck, I took a deep breath and stared at him straight on. He would not intimidate me out of discovering what really happened that night.

"It was you."

"You don't understand." His voice hesitated, so he cleared his throat before continuing. "It was an accident."

He looked at his feet. I could not tell if it was in shame or to try to hide the fact that he was still lying.

"Funny how the police said the 911 call came from some skateboarders," I spat. "I mean, decent people call when there has been an accident, Brett. Murderers flee the scene."

With the last line, the color drained from his face. He looked me in the eye after taking a deep breath of his own. I hoped it was because he was about to tell me the truth.

"You've got it all wrong. It wasn't murder," he said, and sat back down and fumbled through his desk. "We were arguing about the price, and she tripped."

"You mean you pushed her." I put the cufflink in my pocket and took a step closer to his desk. "Just admit it already! There was no offer. Never, and I mean never would Tona even think about selling!"

Too many people had lied to me this week. I could not take hearing yet another excuse from some wannabe hoping to get away with murder.

"It was a mistake," he said, and opened another drawer after not finding what he was looking for in the first. "I never meant to—"

"You know what, Brett? I've had it with this malarky. We'll let William settle this."

I reached for the phone on his desk as he pulled his hand up, holding a gun. Awesome, I was going to die. Azure was right. I was such a tea-tart! What had I been thinking?

Confronting a murderer, real smart, Hailey.

"William won't be deciding anything," he said, and gestured with his gun for me to sit down.

I did as he wanted. My only hope now was to bide my time and hope that help was on the way. He pulled a briefcase out from under the desk and slammed it down on top, trying his best not to take his eyes off me.

"Help," I transmitted to Azure. "It's Brett. He has a gun."

He did not respond. I must have been too far away from him. My body tightened as my heart continued to attempt pounding out of my chest. I just needed to breathe. I could talk myself out of this. Aubrey knew I was here, well, somewhere.

TEA!

Brett sat back down in his chair and fumbled with what I assumed from the sound was some sort of safe.

"I never meant for her to die," Brett pleaded.

"I get it," I said in the most reassuring voice I could muster. "You're not a killer."

"Exactly. It was a giant misunderstanding. She was playing hardball, and we started to argue . . . And she just fell."

He got the safe open and tossed its contents into the briefcase—money, paperwork, and keys. I needed to keep him talking. Maybe my fleeing caused Aubrey to panic. There was no way she just watched me run out of the café and did not call William to spill the truth to him. I took another deep breath. I needed to stay calm. If I kept him talking, everything would be fine. Someone would come for me.

"You left her there to die," I said. Tears wet my eyes.

Do not cry, do not cry.

"How could you walk away from her like that?" I asked.

"It wasn't like that," he said. "There was someone out back, and I panicked. I meant to call 911, but how would I explain what happened? I'm too pretty for prison."

"Brett." I raised my hands as the gun wavered. "Focus."

His eyes were staring at the wall. He could not bring himself to look at me. The gun in his hand trembled. After clearing his throat, he snapped the lid to the briefcase shut.

"I don't want to hurt you, Hailey," he said. A second briefcase slammed onto the desk, causing me to jump. "I just want to pack up and head out of town. Can you let me do that?"

"That's a good plan. Just leave town. Don't come back. You've got a passport, right?" I said. In reality, my mind was screaming, *No, Brett! You cannot leave town! You need to be in jail, not fleeing the country!* But I tried to focus and slow my breathing.

He put his laptop and some other electronics on his desk into the second briefcase.

"Good," he said, looking at me in the eyes. "I'm really sorry about this. I didn't mean—"

As he slung one of the briefcases on his shoulder, there was a loud cracking sound at the front door, and Barry Bear burst into the room, gun drawn.

Out of instinct, Brett swung his gun away from me and to the doorway and fired a shot. I yelped and fell to the ground. When no one screamed out, I looked behind me and saw that the bullet hit the wall beside the doorway. I bet he had never fired a gun before.

By the look on his face, it was clear the firing of the gun was an accident. The color was gone, and he stood in complete shock at what just happened. It surprised me that a second shot did not come from Barry, though I figured they trained him in subduing without having to kill.

For a moment, neither of the men moved. The sheriff's office had not been forced to use their guns in the line of duty in my lifetime. No doubt Barry wanted any other option than to shoot Brett.

"Put the gun down slowly," Barry said in his most commanding voice. He sounded an awful lot like our high school football coach.

Brett looked at Barry, and for a split moment, I feared there would be a shoot-out—like in the old westerns where the sheriff is forced to kill the bad guy—but Brett took a deep breath and slid the gun across the desk. He broke down in tears right there before us. Full-blown waterworks, the kind I thought only existed in old Hollywood films.

"You have the right to remain silent . . ." Barry read Brett his rights as he holstered his gun and retrieved his handcuffs.

The relief flooded out of me in a wave, and I used the distraction to wipe my face clean with my shirt. I needed to pull myself together. Thank the bean it was Barry and not William.

"Barry Bear," I gushed in an effort to hide my fears. "You just saved my life!"

I batted my eyes at him and tried to give him my best innocent pose, but he saw right through it.

"Do you fancy yourself a member of the force, Ms. Morton?"

"No, Mr. Bear." I smiled deeper. "I was just taking out the trash."

He blushed then cleared his throat. "You know full well that my last name isn't Bear."

"And you know full well I would never pose as an officer of the law. I don't think I would look near as good in a uniform."

His blush deepened, but our stare down was interrupted by Brett, pleading for his innocence. The man sure could ruin a moment.

Barry cuffed Brett and led him out of the office, but not before stopping to place his muscular hand on my shoulder. "Are you going to be okay?"

"I think so," I lied. "I have to find Aubrey. I ran—"

"She's at the café. She's the one who called it in. You're lucky William and I were close by."

"Thank you."

"Only doing my job," Barry said. "But you're welcome. We can discuss the sensibility of your actions later."

Brett cried the entire way out. Hopefully, the sleazeball's company, Lake Front Real Estate, would be closed down for good.

I did not even bother to lock the door behind me as I left.

Once at the curb, I could not help but antagonize Brett as Barry shoved him into the back of his car with care for his head.

"Hey Brett!" They looked over at me. "There was never any offer. Tona was just leading you on because you wouldn't stop harassing her."

He let his head fall to his lap. I was not completely sure it was the truth. But knowing Tona, it was something she would do to get back at someone trying to sell to her.

After shutting the door, Barry came back to where I stood.

"Are you sure you're okay? I can drop you at the café if you need me to."

"Barry, I had no idea you cared so much." I gave him a sly smile. "I'm a big girl; I can walk. It's only a block away."

He shook his head and went back to his car. Before opening the door, he met my eyes.

"William is going to want your statement. Do you want me to come by tonight or in the morning?"

"Let's do it tonight," I said with a wink. "I can't imagine I'll be able to sleep. The company would be welcome."

"You're nothing but trouble," he said, shaking his head.

I gave him a shrug and headed back to the café.

Friday, February 21st

Once I made it back to the café, I sent Aubrey home. It took a bit of coaxing, but I assured her I would fill her in after a decent soak in the tub. Barry and William were coming back, anyway. No reason for her to hang around here until then. Her kids needing to get put down for the night was finally the statement that got her to go.

I barely made it up the stairs. My body was not okay with running on nothing but adrenaline and fear for most of the evening. I called out for Azure but got no response.

He must have been out searching for me. Hopefully, he would not be too mad to discover I was already home. I needed to ask him what the range was on our ability to communicate with each other.

Him being out of the house did mean I would be able to bathe in peace. So, I took full advantage of the silence, almost falling asleep in the tub. I was getting dressed when his voice finally filled my mind.

"HAILEY, WHERE ARE YOU!?"

"I'M AT HOME! CRISIS AVERTED. GET BACK HERE FOR STORY TIME."

Okay, maybe I did not need to yell, but it was worth it to feel his side eye and a growl come through the transmission. Who would have guessed that I would miss him interrupting my every thought?

"Just wait until I get back there," Azure transmitted.

I snickered and headed down to the café.

Barry was the first to make it back, and he waited patiently for William and Aubrey to walk in without question. It made my heart sing that he was not trying to get the story out of me first, as my second biggest pet peeve was to explain myself twenty different times.

I made sure everyone had a hot drink—Aunt Tona would have been proud—and then I took a seat with Azure in my lap.

"You're lucky I arrived last. No way would I let you put off explaining yourself," Azure transmitted.

I sent him a rude expression as I cleared my throat to begin.

"First"—I looked at William—"I just want y'all to know that I don't blame you for mishandling my aunt's death.

"If I hadn't been so focused on trying to come to terms with it, I probably wouldn't have thought twice about her cause of death."

William gave me a slight nod.

"The tea you wouldn't have," Azure transmitted.

I cuddled him deeper in response. Everyone sat quietly, waiting for me to continue. I assumed they thought I was getting my grief together, not purposefully loving my dragon that wanted none of it.

"I'm so grateful I filled Aubrey in on my suspicions and that she thought to send y'all after me," I said as I smiled at her. She smiled back and waved me off. "I bet Sam's face was priceless when you showed up, William."

"I definitely gave them a start, barreling in the door like I did," William said. "But this is why you should leave legal matters to the—"

He was cut off by Aubrey elbowing him in the ribs.

I hid my laughs by taking a drink from my mug. My eyes met Barry's, and I blushed. It had to be a crime to be so good-looking. After the week I had, I was thankful he came to hear the statement. Eye candy always made it easier to tell a hard tale.

"Barry Bear, thank you again."

"I'm glad to see you're safe," Barry said. "But I've told you a hundred times. It's Barry or Deputy West."

I held out my wrists to him. "Would you like to handcuff me over it?" I said, with a smile on my face that made him blush.

William choked into his drink. I bet it had been a while since he witnessed decent flirting.

"Anyway?" Aubrey asked.

Watching her squirm with anticipation made my evening.

"Right," I said, still smiling at Barry. "Aunt Tona practically raised me in this café. I've seen her maneuver around the roaster thousands of times. I just had a hard time believing that she fell with enough force to cause her death. She was a graceful woman."

I gave Azure a scratch behind the ear. While his original theory had been completely wrong, it was truly because of his insights into Aunt Tona that I ever began to investigate the matter. Not that I could tell them that I started investigating because my pet cat told me to.

"But the coroner said—" William began.

"That is what I kept telling myself," I said. "It was really just a gut feeling. So many of my encounters this week put up red flags regarding her death. But in the end, it was cleaning out the roaster that solved it for me."

I shifted in my chair. Azure's fat belly was making my leg go numb. He meowed. His way of telling me to sit still.

"Sam and I had a run-in at the market, and he was worse for wear. Tanner told me that Sam and Tona had been lovers. So, my original theory was that Sam did it in a fit of jealous rage."

"Why would he be jealous?" Barry asked. "I didn't know Tona was with anyone."

"Well, it's come to my attention that Tona had an active nightlife." I gave him a smirk. "Apparently, she had one heck of a Valentine's date before the incident."

"I'm still jealous. I want to be a night for the record books," Aubrey said with a pout.

"Hon, you break the record books every night," William said.

I almost fell out of my chair in laughter. His Texas accent made it all the funnier. Aubrey ate it up.

"I'll show you something record-breaking," she said, trying her hardest not to burst into laughter.

"Get a room, y'all," Barry said. "We're trying to take a statement here."

"All right, mister serious," I said, glancing at the love birds.

It was rare for me to hang out with both William and Aubrey. But I adored their playful relationship.

"Back to the story it is." I took a drink before starting again. "So, I only had initials to go on, from the post-Valentine's flowers that arrived for Tona. And Sam Wilcox is the only S.W. I know."

"Plus, Tanner tried to sneak rats in here the other night," Aubrey interjected.

I gave her a look to shut up, but it was too late.

"He did what?" William asked.

"Don't worry about it," I said. "It's under control."

"If you say so."

I gave him a reassuring smile.

"Anyway, Brett wasn't actually on my list as a suspect, really. I thought his pushy visits were to entice me into selling. But when I found a realtor association cufflink in the roaster, I realized what had happened."

I waited for them to jump in with the solution, but they did not.

"What did a cuff link prove?" Barry asked.

"That he fought with Aunt Tona that night," I said, slightly annoyed.

It was clear as day to me. "I knew she had cleaned out the roaster the night of her death."

"I see," Barry said, deep in thought.

"Brett approached me twice this week regarding the café. I can only imagine how many times he had hassled Aunt Tona. Now I can't be one hundred percent sure on exactly what happened—you'll have to ask him—but I think it went something like this.

"Brett upped the offer, and Aunt Tona was tired of arguing with him and being polite the way she was. So, she offered to sell, but for a price that was outrageous. Probably enough for us to retire or open a brand new, larger location. That's just how she was. Always trying to resolve issues with wit instead of arguments.

"I think Brett lost it and started yelling. Aunt Tona, being herself, wouldn't stand for him yelling and tried to push him out the door to leave. They got into a scuffle over there." I pointed to the roaster in the front.

Aubrey and William had to turn their heads to look behind them. Barry Bear nodded his head, as if he could see it all going down in front of his eyes.

"One thing led to another," I continued, "and Brett pushed back. But as she fell, Aunt Tona grabbed hold of his wrist, and that's how the cuff link flew into the roaster."

Everyone seemed impressed with the clue.

"That's tragic," Aubrey said.

"I know," I said. "The saddest part is I believed Brett when he said he never meant to hurt her. We've known him our whole lives. Sure, he acts like he is still one of the frat boys and can be pushy when trying to make a sale, but the man has never so much as been in a bar fight. I do think the whole thing was an accident."

"Why did he run then?" William asked. "Why not call for an ambulance?"

"I think he panicked," I said. "He told me. While he was trying to figure out what to do, there was a sound out back, and he feared being caught in a compromising position. He didn't want to go to jail, so he fled."

"Too late for that," Barry said.

"That was probably me," Azure transmitted, and I could hear the tears in his voice. He curled up tight into my lap.

"So, what happens now?" Aubrey asked.

"Justice," William said.

"It'll be up to the jury and a judge," Barry said. "But I expect Brett will spend a few years in prison."

"Think he'll come back after?" Aubrey asked.

"I sure hope not," I said. "I don't ever want to see him again."

We let the silence fill the room as we sipped on our drinks. The relief of solving both cases this week left me feeling exhausted but also relieved. It was over, I had the answers, and I could rest knowing Tona's last day on Earth was one of the happiest.

"If I'm being honest with y'all, I'm glad the fight happened in front of the windows. I don't think I would have been able to reopen the café if I would have discovered her body the next morning."

"I'll drink to that," Aubrey said. She raised her mug, and everyone followed suit.

"To Tona," Barry said, and we clinked mugs.

After everyone finished their drinks, I let them out and locked up the café.

"Time for dinner!" Azure transmitted as he followed me to the stairs.

"Wow, having a somber moment here," I transmitted. "Is that all you think about?"

"This entire week has been a somber moment," he transmitted. "This somber moment also happens to be dinnertime."

"All right, I'll let it slide."

Once we got upstairs, I filled his bowl with a can of wet salmon meat. To my surprise, he started purring as soon as he took his first bite. "Salmon is my favorite."

"I'll keep that in mind." I walked to the fridge to see if past me saved leftovers. No luck. "I'm starving."

"Order a pizza," Azure transmitted between bites.

We had only lived together for a week, and he was already on top of my eating habits. I was going to have to step up my game.

"I guess, really, I just want to cry or hide from the world. Maybe I just need to sleep for a solid twenty-four hours."

"Eat. It will make you feel better." He let out a loud belch.

"Obviously, it's working wonders for you," I transmitted with a laugh.

I flopped on the couch and looked around the room. This could be home. I did not know what I was so worried about when I feared moving into the apartment earlier in the week.

"I'm glad to hear you say that. I want this to be your home too," Azure transmitted.

He jumped up on the couch next to me and snuggled in as I ordered my favorite pizza: pineapple and salami.

Sunday, February 23rd

After two long nights of crying—that I did not want to get into with anyone—I felt more put together than I had since Tona's death.

Azure and I made our way downstairs to prepare the café for the day. Mornings were going to be the death of me. Thankfully, it was Sunday, which meant a slow start to the day, with a noon rush.

Before I had a chance to open the storeroom door, there was a knock on the front glass. It was barely past 7:00 a.m., so I had no clue as to who in the world would be knocking. I figured it was a tourist who was choosing not to read the sign. The entire town knew we opened at 8:00 a.m.

I peered out of the storeroom door to find Aubrey standing under the awning with a stack of covered trays. I could not recall asking her to come to work, but I rushed over to unlock the door for her.

Had it been a tourist, I would have waited them out in the storeroom. Early birds do not get the coffee.

"Aubrey Rose, what in the tea are you doing here so early? What is all of this?"

I took half of the trays out of her hands as we made our way through the café. I looked over my shoulder as I walked to see Aubrey glowing with joy.

"They're for you," she said. "You mentioned how you wouldn't be able to buy from Tori for a month, so I thought I would help out."

Did I really tell her about that?

It had to have been in passing. My big solution was to buy store-baked items for the month Tori was excommunicated.

I opened the first tray to find a sheet of unbaked cinnamon rolls, and the sweet aroma made my mouth water.

"These smell amazing. Is there anything you can't do?"

"Thank you and probably not," Aubrey said.

"And somehow, you stay so humble," I said.

She smirked and gave a small curtsy.

"All in a day's work," she said as I held the storeroom door open for her with my foot then followed her to the counter beside the fridge.

"William and I had a long talk when we got home Friday night," Aubrey said.

I cringed. "I hope I didn't get you into too much trouble. Tell him I swear I learned my lesson—"

She laughed and shook her head. We slid all but one of the trays into the fridge.

"Not that; about the café," she said.

I raised my eyebrows, eager for where this was going. After having Aubrey help for the week, it was clear that I would have to hire someone, not that I had any idea how I would go about it if she turned me down.

"I'm in!" she about shouted as she threw her arms in the air. "We agreed that it's time I went back to work. That is, if you can afford me?"

"Of course!" I squeaked, while I bounced on the balls of my feet in excitement. "I was hoping to get away with free labor, but since you're going to hardball me. . ."

"Sass before coffee? Girl, don't hurt yourself."

"It's a lifestyle, no fuel required." I winked. "But seriously, I was going to cut you a check yesterday for the week. But it slipped my mind with all that happened. Are you okay with the salary Aunt Tona paid me?"

"Are you sure you can afford that?" she asked.

"I don't see why not," I said. "I have so many ideas for this place. With your help, we could really ramp up business."

She gave me a long hug. Working with her was going to be fantastic.

"How should we celebrate?" I asked.

"Cinnamon rolls and Aconite Affogatos!"

"You read my mind!"

I walked over to the oven and turned it on to preheat.

"By the way," Aubrey said, in a nonchalant tone that made my stomach drop, "I saw the first bluebonnet of the season Friday night when I dropped the kids off at the sitter on my way here."

"The tea you did! What is this, like the fourth year in a row you've seen the first sighting? Not fair."

"Aw, you thought life was fair?"

We burst into laughter.

The morning passed in a blur. Aubrey and I hammered out the finer details of shifts and decided to look for a high school student to help on the weekends. She needed those to spend with her kids and William. In return, I would get to go back to sleeping in.

After cleaning the café for the evening, I erased Oleander Spice from the Poison of the Week board. It was my final send-off to a woman that I aspired to be.

I flipped through my secret book of poisonous drinks and filled in the board for the upcoming week.

Flame Lily Macchiato—an espresso topped with a dollop of foamed milk and a sprinkle of cinnamon candies.

No matter what the week had in store for me, I was ready.

"Yes, yes. You're ready for anything. Now, can you stop with the pep talk so we can get these beans roasted?" Azure transmitted.

I looked over at him, waiting by the roaster. His sapphire scales glistened in the evening sun. A real-life dragon in my café. The world was a funny place.

"This real-life dragon bites," Azure transmitted.

Little did he know, it would be the last time he bit anyone.

"Stop it!" he transmitted.

My thoughts are so fun. Look at me thinking all the random things. I wonder if dragons are ticklish. They have to be. Dogs are. Cats are. I should try to tickle him.

"ALL RIGHT! You've made your point! I will teach you to block your thoughts from me," he transmitted, sounding utterly defeated.

"Thank you. That's all I ask, just a little privacy," I said aloud.

"I was not doing it to hurt you. I needed to know your worth," he transmitted. "The most efficient way to get to know a person is to hear your unfiltered thoughts. You've passed the test."

"Do I get a gold star?"

"Hardly. You get the pleasure of protecting me," he transmitted.

He sat up straight and expanded his wings. While he looked as dignified and pompous as could be, I could not help but double over in laughter. The blank stare he sent through our connection made it worse. It was impossible to take him seriously when he was displaying himself in such a manner. With that thought, he slammed his wings closed.

"You know, we could be upstairs already had you not run out of here in the middle of my roasting lesson," he transmitted.

"Hey now, I was solving the case you did not think I was up to solving on my own!" I transmitted.

"You're just lucky we had extra bags we could open for the weekend customers."

I rolled my eyes and noted his lack of "thank you for catching the killer" as I walked to the storeroom to load a bag of unroasted beans onto a cart to roll to the roaster. There was no way I was going to be hauling a hundred-pound bag of anything, anywhere, without wheels to assist me.

"Weakling," Azure transmitted as I pushed the cart into the café.

"You can do it yourself if you'd like," I transmitted.

"No, no, you are doing a fine job."

"Thank you. About time I get some recognition. So what do I do?"

"Sure, we can call it recognition if it helps you sleep at night," Azure transmitted.

"Funny," I transmitted. I stopped the cart at the roaster and looked down at him. "What's next, Your Highness?"

"All you need to do is follow my instructions. The settings are pre-programmed, so you do not need any actual skills besides listening . . . Though, it seems like that might be a tough one for you."

"Okay, rude. What are you going to do while I am listening?"

"You ask too many questions."

"A dragon is about to roast coffee beans in front of me, so I think it's completely acceptable for me to be curious about the process."

"Fine, fine, I am going to open this door behind the machine." He used his paw to push a button that blended into the back panel, and a door popped open. "Then I will step inside and roast the beans."

My eyes lit up, but before I could ask my next question, he let out a long sigh and shook his head. It made me smile to see him get so worked up over a couple of questions. How else was I expected to learn anything about him?

"This roaster does not have any heating elements, as we do not need them. You will be turning on the system that keeps the beans moving so I can roast them evenly. After I am finished, you will shut off the machine, and we will let them cool before transferring them to packages and tubs."

Out of all the times I had watched Tona roast beans, I never knew Azure was inside the roaster. Her ability to keep secrets was awe-inspiring.

"All in all, how long will this take?"

"Don't ask me questions you already know the answers to. I know full well that Tona taught you the ins and outs of how beans roast."

"Okay, mister grumpy butt, let's get started."

"Finally," he transmitted and stepped inside the roaster.

Over the course of about thirty minutes, I followed each of Azure's requests to the tea. The one thing I would not joke around with was roasting coffee. Whatever he wanted me to do, I would, as long as I got to taste that flavorful bean.

"And we're done," Azure transmitted as he climbed out of the panel and shut it.

"Does that mean I can brew a cup?!" I squealed.

"You're in luck. Typically, you would want the beans to rest for at least twenty-four hours to four days before cupping, but since I am a dragon and roasted them with magic, you can dive in now."

"YES!" I yelled.

The sudden volume of my voice made Azure jump.

"I'm not sure you need any more coffee," Azure transmitted.

He jumped up into an armchair and stretched his back into an arch before settling in for a nap.

"You shh," I said.

"Don't mind if I do."

I grabbed a mug from the counter and scooped out enough beans to brew an espresso. It had been a long time since I had tasted the straight-from-the-roaster flavor.

While the café always smelled like coffee, the newly roasted beans let off an aroma that made my mouth water—a deep, rich smell that I had yet to find a faux candle for. Being able to smell it more often was one benefit I was looking forward to by living in the café.

After it was done, I held the mug under my nose, taking in the experience. A deep breath later, I took a small sip.

Perfection.

The last nine days were some of the worst of my life, but the simple pleasure of drinking freshly roasted coffee melted every inch of tension away. Life could only get better from here.

I looked over at Azure sleeping peacefully at the front of the café. Where I knew how bad my week had been, I could only imagine how terrible his was. I should not have been as hard on him or pushed him to train me as much as I did.

Losing the first one he was ever bonded to was an experience I did not want to live for a long time.

As I drank my espresso, I vowed to myself and Aunt Tona's memory that I would be the best protector I could be.

"You've been a great help to me this week," Azure transmitted in a sleepy tone.

"As you have to me," I transmitted. "We've got to lean on each other to get through this."

"I agree. Thank you for finding Tona's killer," he transmitted.

"You're welcome." I smiled. "We make a great team, if I do say so myself."

"We'll see about that. It's only been a week," he transmitted.

"Only a week? Feels like twenty years," I transmitted with a laugh. I cleaned out my mug and stretched my back. "Ready for dinner?"

"Salmon night?" He mimicked my stretch.

"Maybe. Might have to hold onto those cans. Seems like they will keep you motivated," I laughed as we headed up to the apartment.

"You're not funny," he transmitted.

"All right, all right. Salmon it is."

Author's Biography

Verena DeLuca is a pen name for the life partner duo Sabetha Danes & Nicholi Baldron. When we're not homeschooling our artistic daughter, we spend our afternoons arguing the finer details of books. Failing that, we can be found walking the many nature trails around our home.

Marble Falls is an actual tourist destination, an hour west of Austin, Texas, that we're proud to call home. While Aconite Cafe isn't an actual coffee shop in the town, it is the name of our publishing company. We love coffee nearly as much as Hailey, though we've been known to break the cardinal rule and drink tea.

Azure is based on our cat James, who's just as snarky.

Aconite Cafe

Book & Coffee Connoisseurs

If the coffee doesn't kill you, we have books for that.

Aconite Cafe is a publishing company fueled by coffee. Our Mission is to cure despondency via books.

Our journey began on a lazy Sunday over a cup of coffee. While discussing fantasy books, we joked about opening a coffee shop. That hypothetical business model of a coffeeshop/ bookstore, turned into the dream fueled vision before you; where we read, write, and publish book, all while consuming copious amounts of coffee.

Our love of magical worlds and coffee has since grown into a thriving community of like minded fans.

Cozy Mystery Tribe

STAY IN TOUCH WITH US TO DISCOVER:

Cozy Mystery Books:

- New Releases
- Book Reviews
- Author Interviews

Subscriber Perks:

- Monthly Calendars
- Reading Challenges
- Photo-A-Day Challenges
- Giveaways
- And More!

To Learn more visit us at:

AconiteCafe.com/CozyMysteryTribe

www.ingramcontent.com/pod-product-compliance
Lightning Source LLC
LaVergne TN
LVHW040342231025
824106LV00014B/768
* 9 7 9 8 7 3 0 3 6 5 6 4 3 *